Everything Behind Us

(A Murphy Brothers Story)

The Potter's House Books (Two)

BY
JENNIFER RODEWALD

Everything Behind Us

ISBN: 978-1-7347421-4-5

Any references to events, real people, or real places are used fictitiously. Names, characters, and places are products of the author's imagination, and any similarities to real events are purely accidental.

Front cover image Lightstock.com. Design by Jennifer Rodewald.

First printing edition 2020.
Rooted Publishing
McCook, NE 69001
Email: jen@authorjenrodewald.com
https://authorjenrodewald.com/

For the dads (though I doubt you'll ever read this).
The godly, mighty men of valor.
It's like y'all are superheroes.

The LORD sits enthroned over the flood;
the LORD is enthroned as King forever.
Psalm 29:10 NIV

Chapter One

(in which Sadie returns)

Sadie Allen never intended to return to Sugar Pine.

When she'd been uprooted from home as a confused, broken seventeen-year-old, she had made up her mind. She'd never come back. Like most of her plans, that resolve was now met with failure.

The road into town felt like a haunting dream. One of contradiction—faint hope and strong trepidation. Traveling to the one place she swore she couldn't put herself back in, she found the scene as welcoming as a holiday greeting card, all decorated and delightful and every bit as charming as her memory had kept it. If she didn't know better, she'd never believe there were secrets of tragedy and betrayal kept guarded within this small town.

But she knew better.

Snow lined the plowed street. On the other side of the mounds of white, there was cleared sidewalk, and above that, strands of twinkle lights waved in a gentle evening breeze, hung in a zigzag pattern above the wide walkway. Dressed in winter warmth and generally wearing smiles, people carrying paper bags and wrapped packages strolled beneath the sparkling merriment. A quaint and gentle scene that should be frozen in time. Sugar Pine always did love Christmas, and the town dressed up like it was a feature location for a holiday special. Wreaths on every streetlamp. Garland framing every door. Evergreen swags fancied up with silver bells, and red ribbons hung in storefront windows—all of them likely created by Touch of Home, the up-and-coming local business hatched and owned by Mrs. Helen Murphy.

As Sadie admired the setting with bittersweet longing, her sudden thoughts of Mrs. Murphy threatened an avalanche of devastation. Connor Murphy, Helen's third son, had been at the center of all of it. Though almost nine years post-trauma, Sadie still couldn't bear the thought of facing him. Not any more than she'd been able to dust his memory permanently out of her mind. Likely, that was a product of guilt, and she should accept the hot poker of pain that jabbed her heart every time her thoughts wandered back to that time, to that boy, and to that unamendable mistake. Even so, she'd rather not remember him at all. Just as she'd rather not be driving down this particular street, in this particular town. Especially not with the reason that forced her to return.

The light ahead turned red—one of three traffic lights on this merry Christmas lane. As Sadie's older model Cherokee eased to a stop, the lights made a cheerful glow off the gathering moisture on the silver hood of her car. Everything about this coming-back scene looked on the surface to be enchanting, but it couldn't penetrate the anxiety that snarled through her being. How would she walk down this street again? How could she hold her head up, face the people who had been constant characters throughout her growing-up years? They all knew the story—at least part of it. They all knew how she'd left, and why.

They all had reason not to want her to return.

On her right, the Storm Café's red-and-white-striped awning ruffled in the winter breeze. Light snowflakes twirled to their soft landing as the twinkle lights caught the facets of glitter hidden within their tiny forms. The large windows facing the street had been frosted with painted snow, and someone had carefully etched a sledding scene onto the panes. Such an inviting image would make anyone smile. Anyone but Sadie, and possibly Connor. But she didn't know that for a fact—not for him. Perhaps such things didn't disturb him the way they did her.

As she continued to wait for the stoplight to change from red to green, the door to the café swung open. Her breath caught as the man coming out turned. Tall, sandy-brown hair cut military-style, a firm chin, and deep-set eyes. She knew, even before his profile became a front shot, who he was. She hadn't forgotten the exact shade of the rich forest-green eyes that set him apart from most of his brothers or the firm, more serious line of his mouth that also made him stand out from the other Murphy boys.

With a sharp breath, she diverted her gaze back to the street, tapping her steering wheel with her thumbs and working to steady the pulse that had leapt to a charge. Connor Murphy must be on leave, and she prayed he didn't take in his surroundings the way he used to.

Forcing her mind from the past, Sadie glanced at her rearview mirror. In the corner, slumped against the car door, reflected the one and only reason that could push her back into the place of all her regrets. Dark lashes fanned against adorably chubby cheeks, and his little chest puffed out and then in with each quiet breath. Nearly white hair scattered over his forehead, some of it sticking to his skin.

Ah, Reid. Sleep, my boy, sleep. For him, Sadie would do anything. Everything.

Finally, the light flicked to green, and she continued on her way through town. Two turns up on the highway before the road began to climb the hills, and she'd be where she'd forced herself to go. Mom and Dad were expecting her. It was Mom, in fact, who had convinced her this was not only necessary but for the best. Bless her stubborn love.

Reid needed an anchor for the future, and the recent proclamation from Sadie's doctor compelled her to bring him back to Sugar Pine. Back to the home of her childhood, the seat of her deepest hurts and regrets. For the love of her four-year-old son, she'd face the stage of her past. Because the truth was, she'd run out of options. She had nowhere else to go.

***

"You okay, son?"

With a small jolt, he righted his posture and dipped a rushed nod. Connor Murphy wasn't one to let himself get sidetracked. He was a man of purpose, one who kept moving, who did the next thing. Which was likely why standing in the middle of the sidewalk as if he'd been run off-course struck his father as odd.

"Yes, sir." Connor motioned up the street, struggling to reassemble his meticulously kept, orderly thoughts that, in a glance, had just been scattered like snowflakes in a gust of wind. "Lead on. Jackson and I will follow."

"Looked like you got lost for a second," Dad said.

Connor molded a grin that felt like wax. "No, sir. Just enjoying this Christmas snow."

How could a glimpse inflict this much of a response? He didn't even know for certain the woman had been her.

No. Without a doubt, he knew.

Though he followed his dad, Jackson now striding at his side, Connor's mind wouldn't leave the woman he'd just spotted in a late '90s Jeep Cherokee—the reason his father had caught him standing, staring into the street like his world had been turned inside out yet again. Had it really been her? With a glance over his shoulder, he tried to glimpse her face beyond the gleam of water and light on her windshield.

The light turned green, and the Jeep rolled forward. The woman driving it didn't glance back at him, but his gut instinct didn't waver. He didn't need her to look back to know for certain who she'd been. He hadn't seen her in nine years—though there hadn't been a day during that time that he hadn't lifted a painful supplication to heaven on her behalf.

Connor had begged God for her healing. Her stability. And for her forgiveness. But he'd never believed he'd see Sadie Allen again.

Chapter Two

(in which Connor decides to face Sadie)

Home hadn't changed a whole lot, but it felt strange to be there, to wake up in her childhood bedroom, and to wander through the floorplan that had been all she'd known for all her growing-up years.

Sadie wrapped the oatmeal-colored cable-knit sweater around her, swaddling herself against the predawn chill. These days she had a tendency to stay cold once she got chilled, and it made the ache in her back hard to bear. At the soft feel of the oversized garment, she smiled and brought the gathered bunch of material to her face. It'd been a kind welcome to have her mother drape it around her the evening before. At the memory of that interchange, tears pricked her eyes.

"It's so good to see you here, Sadie." Mom had slipped onto the couch beside her, handing a mug of steaming ginger tea across the space. "All this time I carried a wispy hope that someday you'd find your way back."

It hadn't been that Sadie had lost the way home. It was that the life she'd left behind had been too full of mistakes to face. Still, Sadie understood what Mom meant, and she'd pressed her mouth up into a small smile.

"I'm sorry the years have been hard for you, Mom."

"Oh dear, don't misread me. I know why you've stayed away, and your dad and I haven't minded traveling to see you and Reid." Mom's attention drifted toward the wall where Sadie's senior picture still hung in a frame. Next to it was a smiling Reid—the photo taken the spring before. Mom sighed. "I just wish there could be reconciliation for you."

A tremor rolled through Sadie, and she shut her eyes against the haunting gust of past sins. Mom turned her head back to her and saw her shiver.

"Are you cold?" Mom slipped off the bulky sweater that had swathed her frame and settled it around Sadie's thin shoulders.

It had been warm from Mom and smelled of ginger and cinnamon.

"There now," Mom said, buttoning the top oversized button. "It's like wearing a blanket wherever you go."

From there, the evening had been quiet. Nana and Pops, as Reid called Sadie's parents, had a Christmas Eve gift for their only grandson to open—a new pair of Paw Patrol jammies—and then Pops indulged the four-year-old in a game of Candyland before bedtime. After Sadie had her son snuggly tucked into the cot Dad had set up in her room for him, she came back out to the family room to say good night, carrying the sweater.

Mom waved her away as Sadie reached to hand it back.

"Keep it, sweetie. The color makes your blue eyes shine, and it will keep the winter draft from seeping in."

In the new morning hours of Christmas, Sadie inhaled the scent of her mom still lingering in the yarn of the garment. While the electric teakettle heated water, she stood at an east-facing window that framed a view of the coming sunrise over the evergreen treetops. As she watched the first gentle wisps of light chase away the December night, she sniffed. Christmas morning. Her first spent at home in nine years. A tear leaked from one eye and ran down the length of her nose, and she used a sleeve to dab the wetness away. The feel of that cable knit against her skin provoked a tiny shudder and several more rolling tears.

It wasn't that Sadie had needed a sweater—she had three in the suitcase she still needed to unpack. Her emotional response to her mother's simple gesture went so much deeper.

They'd never condemned her. Hadn't rejected her—even though for a brief time when she'd been eighteen, she'd felt it to be so. For all of her blundering through life and the heartache she'd caused them—and goodness, had she caused them a lot—they ever loved her.

Gratitude and unworthiness stirred a poignant response from her soul. Especially since now, more than ever before, she needed them. Reid needed them.

Sadie shut her eyes, though the sunrise was now displaying the peak of its splendor. Cervical cancer. How? Why? She was barely twenty-seven...

Anxiety wound through her as she thought of Reid, of her parents, and of the future. Mom and Dad had been in their late thirties when they'd met and married and past forty when she'd joined their little family. In three months Dad would be seventy-one. That summer, Mom would turn sixty-nine.

If the worst was true, as the doctor in Nevada had feared, where did that leave all of them? How were her aging parents going to raise her four-year-old son if she couldn't beat the cancer?

Maybe I'll beat the odds... The thought fell flat in her heart. While she could cling to that thin hope for day-to-day existence, she couldn't bank on it long term. Not for Reid. It would be irresponsible, and she'd been irresponsible long enough in her life.

The distant sound of bells tolling in town summoned Sadie's attention away from her inward gloom. A bright yellow-orange glow smeared across the horizon now; the sun had claimed victory once again. The beauty of the valley sunrise pulled a soft smile to her lips, and then an arm slipped around her shoulders.

"I heard the bells on Christmas day, on Christmas day..." Mom leaned in and sang the carol softly against Sadie's ear, just as she had when Sadie was a little girl.

Back then she'd been a bundle of excitement as she'd waited for the sun to rise. *Soon*, her girlish self would whisper. Soon, the sun would rise, Christmas would come, and with it a smattering of joy that would be enough to fuel the new year. Then the bells at St. Anne's church would toll, every year ringing in the dawn of that most glorious day with the same carol. And then Mom would be there, scooping Sadie up and singing near her ear.

"...so early in the morning," Sadie sang back to her mom, past the pasty dryness of her throat.

Mom wrapped her other arm around her and gently squeezed Sadie's shoulders. "Merry Christmas, my sweet daughter."

Sadie laid a hand on Mom's arm and leaned against the woman who had held her on so many Christmas mornings. "Merry Christmas, Mom."

A beat went by, and then Mom sniffed. "This is the perfect gift. To have you home."

***

Christmas morning had been the usual brand of Murphy chaos. Connor took it all in his normal way. He watched quietly, chuckled often, and when appropriate, took part in the antics that were part of life in a big family of boys. Comfortably tucked beside his younger brother Tyler into the corner of Mom's shabby-chic sofa, hot mug of homemade mocha near his hand, Connor noticed the shakiness of Tyler's hands. Perhaps a lingering issue from the injury his younger brother had suffered after a fall on a job he'd worked with Dad over the previous fall break. As a nudge of concern wove through him, Connor silently lifted a prayer for Tyler's recovery.

Across the room, he also grinned at the way Matt fawned over his wife. They'd announced their pregnancy over breakfast that morning, and the glow between the couple was unmistakable. As he rejoiced in his brother and sister-in-law's good news, part of Connor was relieved that Jacob and Kate hadn't made it home this year. Matt and Lauren's announcement would have cut into Jacob and Kate like a razor, though Connor suspected that most of their brothers were unaware of the struggles their stiffer and more standoffish brother was wrestling with.

He also observed Jackson and Mackenzie and their glowing newfound love for each other. Simply amazing. His younger brother was himself, but also, was not. Jackson laughed and teased as always—family prankster that he was—but was warmly tender with Mackenzie. He seemed more settled, like he didn't feel like he needed to prove something, as he doted on his infant daughter. They were a miracle, and knowing how amazing it was that Jackson and Mackenzie had found this joy in their marriage was powerful. Watching them revived the reason Connor hadn't slept much the night before.

The year before, Jackson had said something that penetrated Connor's mind and heart, and that memory had come on strong and relentless. When Connor had questioned Jackson bringing Mackenzie home for Christmas last year, pretending they had marriage of love and not a mistake of gargantuan proportions, Jackson had come back with a simple response. *What if it could be?*

Love. That was what his brother had been driving at. What if Jackson's marriage could work because his younger brother was committed to it? What if it could become a relationship of love because of his determination for it?

That response didn't fully sink into Connor's mind, his soul, until yesterday. Until he'd spotted Sadie Allen. The words had played chase with his emotions until late at night, when Connor's thoughts settled on Sadie in the dark stillness of the house. How could something said a year past suddenly carry such weight?

In the rare quiet that only seemed to occur in the Murphy home during the dead of night, Connor couldn't get Jackson's earnest response from his mind. Nor could he brush away the image of Sadie's profile as she'd waited for the stoplight to turn green.

For lack of sleep, and of peace, Connor had prayed for Sadie Allen. And for wisdom to understand this mystery that had woven the events of the day so tightly together in Connor's mind.

He'd written to Sadie once, many years back, after they'd both moved away from Sugar Pine. He'd just finished his tech training at Kessler AFB in Mississippi and had been assigned to Germany for a two-year tour. After his time in basics, and then tech school, he still hadn't been able to shake the impression that he needed to reach out to her, so he had. His letter had been honest, the words hard to put down. But necessary, because he'd needed to apologize to her. Two weeks after he'd sent his written apology as a nineteen-year-old young man whose shoulders couldn't bear the burden of everything, his hand-addressed envelope had come back, unopened.

Return to sender.

He'd never tried to reach her again, understanding that she wanted a clean break, a chance to start over, to find life anew. He got it, more than anyone else possibly could.

For him, however, that hope for a clean slate wasn't possible. The memories would always be with him, and he'd accepted it. His life would be forever marred by that winter their senior year, and he used the burden of responsibility to fuel his life and devotion. Connor had always carried responsibility like it was ordained cargo, but after the mistakes that led to Ivy's death and Sadie's departure, that sense of responsibility became his determination to live a life of honorable duty. To serve, to live well, and to take care of those whom God would entrust to him.

And to pray for Sadie.

It'd been nine years, and now she'd come back. Throughout the previous night, every time that thought echoed, Connor had found that his chest pained, his breath labored.

Why had she returned?

Sadie wouldn't come back to Sugar Pine unless she had a good reason. Actually, something told Connor that her reason was one of desperation, which wasn't good at all. And the same intuition hinted that he'd witnessed her return intentionally—there was a cause for her homecoming that he was duty bound to discover.

Even as he sat amid the madness that was a Murphy Christmas, that feeling of responsibility smoldered through him, branding a resolve in his mind. He'd go see the Allens tomorrow, as he always did when he was home, with a bouquet of Mom's making as his offering of repentance and continued loyalty to Sadie's family.

This year, though, Sadie would be there. After all this time, he'd stand before her face to face. Maybe now, finally, she would be ready to hear his apology. And he'd find out why she'd come home.

Chapter Three

(in which Connor meets Reid)

Cinnamon rolls were traditionally on the breakfast menu the day after Christmas. Sadie inhaled the yummy aroma of fresh bread and cinnamon as she plucked a promising piece from the table. Tuff yipped out front, the mutt's sharp bark much bigger than the dog himself. Mom chuckled as she scooted her chair away from the card table, laying down the tiny piece she'd been trying to match beside the completed frame of their puzzle.

Some things didn't change, and the Christmas puzzle ritual was one of them. Sadie smiled. She'd always enjoyed the quiet togetherness the activity had provided, and this homecoming year was no different.

The small dog's racket continued to sound, now coming nearer to the front door. Her parents hadn't had a dog when she'd lived at home. Mom had allergies and didn't want pets.

"Tuff Stuff is an outdoor guy, and he needed a home," Mom had explained when Sadie first encountered the energetic, big-personality small dog. Apparently he'd shown up at their door, a lost, wet mess during a spring storm five years back, and no one had known where he belonged. After several weeks of inquiry that led to nothing at all, Mom and Dad had accepted Tuff as a new member of their family.

The pup had been good for them, and Sadie was grateful they had someone on whom they could pour out their warm and generous love.

Mom reached the front door to open it, still laughing. "Tuff, you big noisy thing." Then she paused, a look of realization crossing her features, and her merriment faded.

"Something wrong?" Sadie pushed back on her chair to rise.

"No, nothing." Mom's forced cheery response came way too fast for it to be the truth.

"Who's at the door?" Seemed like a strange question even as Sadie asked it, considering Mom hadn't opened the entry to find out.

Mom inhaled and met Sadie's eyes. For a half a breath, a seriousness Sadie didn't comprehend hung between them. It felt like a warning. Or perhaps a plea. Then Mom fashioned a small smile that failed to light her eyes and returned to the business of the door. Without a response to Sadie, Mom swung open the entry and stepped onto the front deck.

"Tuff, that's quite enough. Connor is not here to attack us."

Sadie froze, her heart crashing into a painful stall. Connor? Connor Murphy? She'd made it no farther than to stand beside the card table, and she found that she'd been rendered immobile in a world that spun around her.

"Good morning, Mrs. Allen." A deep, quiet voice reached Sadie's hearing. The sound of it was vaguely familiar, yet changed. Nine years would do that to a teenager who was now a full-grown man. "Merry Christmas."

Gooseflesh rippled along Sadie's arm as she imagined why Connor Murphy would be at her parents' house.

"Merry Christmas to you too, Connor." Mom's cheerful greeting held unmistakable strain. "Please come in."

"Thank you, ma'am." A hollow clomping sound filled the space as Connor must have stomped his feet. "Sure smells good in here."

And then he was there. All six-foot-four inches of him, wearing a hooded US Air Force sweatshirt, sporting his sandy-brown hair in a groomed military cut, turning those dark-green eyes to her. Sadie held her breath.

"Sadie." His lips closed after he breathed her name, and he stilled, his intense stare pinned on her.

Sometimes she'd wondered what it would be like to see him again. Would the girlish crush she'd had on him since they were eight make her heart mushy? Or would regret make her want to disappear? What would he say, do? What did he think of her now, after everything?

She felt mostly numb. And by his silence, he didn't know what to think or do either.

The strength of his study eased, and the expression he wore moved toward unreadable neutrality. "I thought that might have been you driving through town the other day. Still in your old Jeep?"

Finding her way back to the present, she blinked and then nodded. "Yes. It was probably me."

He nodded, and the discomfort of not know what to say returned to them both. Instead of swimming in it, Connor turned to her mom, extending a Christmas bouquet of white roses, red berries, and evergreen boughs.

"You always bring us such beauties." Mom accepted his offer. "But you must know we don't expect it."

Connor had brought Mom flowers before?

"Yes, ma'am. But I want to." He untucked a rectangular tin from beneath his arm. "Mom sent her homemade hot cocoa mix. She says to tell you Merry Christmas."

"Helen is so kind." Mom moved from the entryway to the open kitchen, waving Connor to follow her. "You'll tell her thank you and Merry Christmas from us, won't you?"

"Of course."

Mom settled the bouquet that certainly Mrs. Murphy had created in a glass vase she'd pulled down from a cabinet and pointed to the counter near the electric teakettle. "You'll stay to sample your mom's hot chocolate?"

They seemed stiffly comfortable together—if that was a thing. As if, sans her own presence in the room, Connor and Mom would have conversed with easy familiarity.

"No, ma'am." Connor placed the tin beside the kettle. "I mean, I don't want to interrupt Sadie's visit. It's been so long..." His attention traveled back to her.

"You aren't interrupting. Is he, Sadie?"

Sadie felt like a mouse with her tail caught in a trap. She could run, but it'd be awful tricky and uncomfortable. She hoped the thing she did with her mouth looked like a smile. "Not at all."

Rolling his shoulders back, Connor's unreadable expression folded a bit at the eyebrows. Was he reconsidering? *Oh no.* What would she do if he did stay? He was sure to ask questions—normal ones, like *Where have you been?* and *What's new in your life?*

She wasn't prepared to chitchat about the past or the present. Didn't Connor know insincere civility when he saw it?

The timer on the oven chimed, and Mom moved toward it, patting Connor's arm as he stepped out of her way. "There now, perfect timing. The rolls are done. You must stay and have one with us and tell us about life. Have you decided if you'll renew your contract this spring?"

Connor visibly swallowed, then turned his gaze back to Sadie. "Are you sure it's okay?" His quiet question was for her alone, and the humble uncertainty in his voice wrapped her heart with an uncomfortable tenderness.

Mom and Dad rarely spoke about Connor to her, but on the occasional mention of him, they'd shared that he'd enlisted in the air force after graduation. That he'd been stationed in Germany after basics, and more recently, he'd been transferred to an air base within two hours of Sugar Pine. She knew from the rare comment concerning him that Connor had kept in touch with them intentionally, and his faithfulness in doing so meant a great deal to them.

For that alone, she could hardly send him straight back out the door.

"Of course. You should stay." Her core quivered even as she said the words.

The corners of his eyes crinkled slightly, the only readable indication of his reaction as he dipped an impassive nod. "Well then."

The front door burst open, causing Sadie to startle and Connor to whip his attention back around to the entry. Sadie barely had a chance to take a fortifying breath before Reid flew into the family room, his arms flailing with pure little boy excitement.

“Pops took me to see where the beavers make their dam! And guess what?” He barely stopped before he collided against her legs, and then he hopped in place, his snow boots dropping clumps of white all over the wood floor. “Just guess!”

“What?” Sadie knelt to unzip his coat.

“I. Saw. One.” Reid leaned in and placed a freezing little palm on either side of her face. “I saw a *beaver*!”

Dad’s chipper laugh rolled from the entry. “We sure did. Right there by their lodge.”

“Are they still on the west side of the meadow?” Connor reached to shake Dad’s hand.

“Yep. Same as always.” Dad pulled Connor into a one-armed hug. “Merry Christmas, young man. It’s good to see you.”

“Yes, sir, you too.” Connor smacked Dad’s shoulder and turned back to the little boy, who now stood sock footed in the kitchen. “And who would this be?”

“I’m Reid. Reid Samuel Allen. Samuel is for Pops.” His pudgy hand lifted with one finger pointed toward Mr. Allen.

“I see.”

Sadie swallowed, wondering if she was supposed to say anything or if she could simply fade against the stone fireplace near the spot where she’d laid out Reid’s coat and boots to dry on the hearth.

“Who are you?” Reid asked.

“Connor Murphy.”

“Sergeant Connor Murphy.” The pride in Dad’s eyes was unmistakable as he stepped beside Connor.

Reid’s eyes widened as he stiffened his posture. “You in the army?”

“No. Air force.”

Sadie’s son smiled broadly and lifted a salute.

“No need for that.” Connor knelt and offered a handshake to the little boy, who took it with the bouncing eagerness of a kid who’d just discovered his new favorite hero. “It’s nice to meet you, Reid Samuel Allen.” He pivoted slightly and pointed toward Sadie. “Is that your mama?”

Her heart clenched. Not because she didn’t want to claim

Reid—she adored her little boy. And not because she'd thought Connor wouldn't figure it out. Sadie was an only child, and Reid called her dad Pops and had stated that he'd been named for him. Of course Connor figured it out. But her breath caught anyway, and Connor's attention came back to her.

"Yep. That's my mommy, Mr. Sergeant Connor. Do you know her?"

"I do." Connor's eyes didn't sway from hers. His pause felt weighted. "She's a friend. One I've prayed for for a long time."

***

"Would you be willing to take a walk with me?" Connor kept his tone low, wanting his request to remain between them for the time being. He'd recognized his opportunity as he and Sadie had a moment alone together at the table after the gathering had shared cinnamon rolls and hot drinks. Mr. Allen had then swooped Reid up from his chair, and together they'd landed on the nearby family room floor in front of the fire. Mrs. Allen had also risen, gathering plates as she moved and waving off both Sadie and Connor as they'd offered to help with dishes.

It was almost as if Mr. and Mrs. Allen had wanted Connor and Sadie to have a few moments to themselves. Feeling unworthy but grateful, Connor took the opportunity.

Sadie studied him openly, a battle clear in her furrowed brow. "How cold is it out there?" Hesitation minced her question.

"Not bad. Pretty nice, actually. I was fine in my sweatshirt coming over here. But if you're not up for it, it's okay." Connor rubbed the edge of his jaw, his two-day beard feeling strangely rough against his palm. He normally shaved twice a day, except when he was on leave. "I just have some things I'd like to say to you, if you're willing to listen. It'd be...easier without an audience." By the painful way his pulse strummed, that claim was only marginally true. The conversation ahead wouldn't be easy either way. Seemed that was often true of things that were necessary.

Sadie's frown softened, though a wariness remained in her eyes. "I'm willing," she whispered. It appeared that she was building up her own courage, fortifying herself for whatever was to come. Then she pressed the corners of her mouth into a small smile. "Give me a few minutes to get my boots and coat."

Nodding, Connor wondered why she'd ignored his claim that it was sweatshirt weather out. He shouldn't be surprised she found him untrustworthy though. He'd proven himself to be so with her, and an extended absence wasn't going to erase that memory.

With her oversized sweater gathered close at her waist, Sadie wandered into the family room, which was only separated by the large leather couch between the dining table and the fireplace. She stopped in front of the hearth and bent to kiss Reid's fair hair as he played with a firetruck Connor guessed had been a Christmas present. "Be good for Pops and Nana. I'll be back in just a bit."

Tipping his head, Reid's expression squished. "Where are you going?"

"For a quick walk." Sadie turned her attention to her mom. "It's okay if I leave Reid with you, right?"

"Of course." Mrs. Allen wandered to Sadie's side and slipped an arm around her slender waist. "I'll have a hot cup of tea ready for you when you get back."

The tenderness between mother and daughter played havoc on Connor's emotions. The pair had always been close, and he knew that sending Sadie away had wrecked Mrs. Allen's heart. The fact that Sadie had stayed away had also been extraordinarily difficult for the gentle woman. Seeing the bond of love still alive and well between mother and daughter offered him a small balm against his frayed conscience.

In that bulky sweater, Sadie had seemed small, but now, with her mother right beside her, Sadie looked tiny. Too slender. Mrs. Allen was an average woman in her late sixties, but it seemed she dwarfed the daughter at her side.

There was something off. As an alarm nudged in Connor's gut, he wondered again what had brought Sadie home, and on the heels of that question, he took in not only her fragile frame but her pallor.

She's sick, isn't she, Lord?

That unease grew into a hard twist in his gut, especially when his attention fell to Reid. The boy met his glance and cocked his head to one side. "Is Mr. Sergeant Connor going for a walk too?"

"He is," Sadie said.

In one quick jump, the kid was on his feet. "Then I go too!"

Sadie wove her fingers through Reid's white hair. "Not this time, buddy."

Those small shoulders sagged, tugging on Connor's sympathy and widening that painful hole in his stomach. "How about if you and I play a round of dominos when I get back?"

"Dominos?" His small nose wrinkled. "That's pizza, Mr. Sergeant Connor. We don't play with food."

Chuckling, Connor squatted in front of Reid, taking in his dark-brown eyes, the bend of his thin lips—more prone to seriousness than mischief—and the curve of his face. He had his mother's keen look of intelligence, even if the color of his eyes were nothing like Sadie's. Hers were sky blue. Connor looked for other traces of Sadie written on her son.

That seriousness, it was her. She had often been mistaken for implacable because of her tendency toward solemnness. He knew that wasn't true of her real personality. Sadie was quiet and deep thinking, but she had also been kind and possessed a gentle spirit—one that was easily nicked by the thoughtlessness of others.

One that he had shamefully overrun.

A driving determination to protect Reid from any such fate gripped Connor, and as impractical and random as it might have been, he welcomed it. Where he had failed Sadie miserably, perhaps he could atone for with Reid.

"I'll teach you the game," Connor said. "If you'd like?"

That serious gaze pinned on him eased into a tiny smile, and Reid nodded. As Connor rolled a fist and held it up for a bump, something fierce and possessive gripped his heart. He and Reid Allen would become friends. And whatever Sadie needed for her son, Connor Murphy was determined to provide.

Chapter Four

(in which Sadie walks with Connor)

The sun shimmered off the freshly gathered snow, its rays warm against her neck. Still, Sadie snuggled into her winter parka, her mittened hands clasping the neck closed to keep away any errant drafts. For many paces, an awkward quiet lingered between Connor and herself, and she wrestled with a desire to fill the space with something that would impress him. It was an historical issue with her—had been nearly an obsession when she'd been an infatuated teenage girl—this drive to gain Connor Murphy's everlasting attention. To make his green eyes settle on her the way they had on Ivy Levens.

It'd been a need that had seen her into trouble and plenty of heartache. Now, many years later, and wiser for the burdens she bore, Sadie smothered that old desire and walked beside him with disciplined silence.

Connor kicked at the gravel road, exposed by the plow that had come through earlier that morning. "I was shocked to see you drive through town the other day."

She glanced at him. Both hands shoved into his pockets, he met her look, his brow furrowed as if pained.

"It's been such a long time since you've been home."

Her gaze drifted from his face, as she didn't want to watch the questions play across his eyes. Nor did she want his guilt. For the past nine years, she'd wanted freedom. Absolution from the wayward footsteps she'd taken. She'd been desperate for some kind of release from the pain and the regret—and she'd fallen into several deep pits looking for a back door out of despair. What she'd found was rock bottom. Total darkness and unparalleled loneliness.

"It has been. Nine years, to be exact." Her breath puffed white in the bright sun.

She'd also discovered in that pit of despair the true amazement of grace. That of her parents, as they continued to love her through all of her misbegotten choices. And then of God, as He'd gifted her with Reid despite the reckless way she'd gotten pregnant with him. If ever she needed real proof that God brought blessings even into the most undeserving situations, she had Reid.

They reached a bend in the road that, if they followed it, would take them toward a trailhead that had been popular among their peers. Up Sugar Pine Creek trail, they'd find the meadows where her dad had taken Reid that morning. Farther back were the upper falls. Above that landmark, after a climb, was another pond and a favorite sledding hill. The theater of much of her childhood and teen years.

And the scene where her life had fallen apart.

Connor paused and reached his ungloved hand to gently clasp her elbow. He waited not only for her attention to turn up to him but for her to turn to match his stance. "I meant what I told Reid. I've prayed for you. Often."

At the onslaught of emotion—both because of his sincere tone and because she'd repressed so many of those past moments and now they came charging back—Sadie blinked and found herself fighting a hard swell in her throat. "Thank you," she croaked. "It was kind of you to think of me."

"Every day, Sadie. I've thought of you every day since you left."

"No doubt wondering if the rumors were true."

"Which rumors?"

A harsh laugh exited her chest. "Yes, indeed. Which ones? I'm sure there were options." She rolled her lips together and then bit the bottom one. Finding his look holding steady on her again, sincerely pleading with her—though for what she wasn't sure—she braced her posture. "I tried to kill myself. Took a full bottle of Oxy I'd found from my dad's knee replacement. And on top of that, drank as much tequila as it took to pass out. Seems that was considered a *true attempt* and not just a cry for help—or something. I don't know exactly what the doctors told Mom and Dad, but it was enough to terrify them. They sent me to a recovery center. A place for healing and hope—that was their tagline."

"Where?"

"In Nevada."

"But...but for nine years?"

"I didn't stay eight months." She crossed her arms over her chest, anchoring her hands on her shoulders. "As soon as I was eighteen and could sign myself out, I left."

Connor's mouth seamed, and his expression grew more pained. "Then what?"

"Then...I did whatever I could." Heat raced through her body, collecting in her face. "Connor, I promise you—you don't really want to know."

A sheen glazed his eyes, and he lifted his chin, his gaze wandering to the tips of the evergreens behind her. By the movement in his neck, he'd swallowed hard. Sadie drew a breath, then reached to cover his sweatshirted arm. "I'm not sure what you're thinking right now, but if this is held-over guilt, I'm asking you to let it go. There are things in my life—in my history—that I'm not proud of, but you're not responsible for them. I made choices."

"So did I." He took a half step nearer, his tall frame towering over her in a way that felt so familiar and protective. Connor searched her face again and gripped her shoulder, this time with a touch of desperation. "That's why I wanted to talk to you. I'm glad you came back. I've needed to tell you how sorry I am."

Nine years was a long time for a young man to carry that kind of burden. Especially when it wasn't his to bear. He'd misunderstood so much, taken responsibility where he shouldn't have. Wanting him to finally find relief, Sadie reached to brush her fingers down the line of his jaw.

"So much weight, Connor."

He blinked.

"It's not yours. You are not responsible for my choices."

"But—"

"I wasn't as innocent as you assume."

"Sadie..."

She cupped his face. "Trust me when I tell you this. My life failures are not your fault. Put that agony to death now. And anyway, the long path of bad choice after bad choice has led me back home. With Reid. There is good in that."

With lines carving the space between his nose and that sheen still shimmering in his green eyes, Connor nodded. "He seems like a good boy."

"He's my gift of grace." Sadie smiled as she dropped her hand, stepping back to a less intimate distance from him.

"Where is his father?"

"I have no idea."

"Does he know about Reid?"

"He does." Sadie turned back toward home and began meandering down the road. "Didn't want anything to do with fatherhood though. We are better off without him."

Matching her easy pace, Connor stepped beside her. "Is that why you came back?"

Saying yes and leaving it at that would be easy, and given that she'd wanted to ease Connor's mind about her, it seemed logical too. But a craving widened within her, needing for at least one person, other than her parents, to know the truth. More specifically, for Connor Murphy to know. Near the mouth of her driveway, she stopped and tipped her face back up to him.

"You've been praying for me?"

"Yes," he breathed.

"Then can I ask you to continue to do so?"

"Of course." His lips parted as his features twisted with concern. When she didn't say more, he slipped a half step closer. "What is it?"

"I'm sick, Connor." Suddenly her voice wouldn't work, and she couldn't tame a rush of tears.

"Sadie..." Her name on his breath was an ache that seemed both unfair and beautiful. And then...

Then she was gathered against his chest, held securely in Connor Murphy's arms. Once upon a time, that was all she had wanted in the world.

***

Sadie shook against him, her muffled cries heartbreaking. Connor felt stunned and cold, as if he'd fallen through the ice at the pond. His lungs ached as he fought against a swelling need to cry himself. He kept her tucked in close, one hand cradling her stocking-capped head, until she sniffed, and he felt the long exhale of a deep sigh leave her frame.

"Can you tell me?" He leaned back, palm still against the blue knit hat covering her long honey-brown hair.

Her eyes remained shut for another beat, but she nodded. After another sniff and a swipe over her tears with her mitten, she looked at him. "I thought I was just rundown—I was so tired all the time, and I started losing weight."

Dropping his hand from her head, Connor nodded. He'd been right—she was awfully thin, unhealthily so.

"But then my back started hurting, and...well, other things started being...not normal." Her winter-air-tinted cheeks flushed into a crimson bloom. "So I finally went to a doctor. I should have gone much sooner..."

"Cancer?"

She dropped her face toward the ground and nodded. "Cervical Cancer."

Dazed, Connor stared at her. She was standing there with him, in the flesh. He'd seen her chuckle with Reid, squeeze her mother's shoulders, banter with her dad. How could this be real? Sure, she looked on the sickly side, but...but cancer? Sadie was only twenty-seven. She should be planning her next vacation, plotting her next career move. Dreaming of marriage and a long, beautiful road through so-happy-together.

Sadie had so much life in front of her. And a son. What of her little boy? This just couldn't be.

Shaking his head, Connor felt a burn of anger roll through

him. "But you're so young."

With a helpless shrug, she breathed a humorless laugh. "Seems the big Mr. C doesn't care."

"But it's treatable, right?" Had to be. Cancer was more treatable now than ever. And Sadie was so young, so...

She pulled her focus back up to him, now composed. "The doctor said it doesn't look good. I hadn't been to a clinic since Reid was born. And I've had HPV—a consequence of being young and careless. The initial tests suggest..." Sighing, Sadie let her gaze drift from him, slowly wandering back to the house.

Back to her son, Connor was sure.

"I'll go to a specialist next week for a second opinion. Then we'll know more."

Her tone came out as if from a recording, so removed. So...clinical. As if she were going in for a routine checkup, just part of everyday life. Run to the store, grab some milk. Pick up her son. Read him a story. Tuck him in. Close out another ordinary day...

Go to the clinic. Find out if she'd live or die.

His gut throbbed as if he'd taken a low blow, and he rolled his fists against the trembling of his fingers.

"What can I do?" He needed to do something. Every honor-driven part of his heart and mind demanded action.

Sadie gripped his hand and squeezed. "Pray for us."

"Yes, but—"

"That's all you can do, Connor. It's not in my hands, and it's not in yours. So pray." She held him with a steady look. There was sadness and resignation in her blue eyes, and it made him want to cry. When she spoke again, her voice was edged with tightness, as if she was clinging onto something for dear life. "After all, God is still King."

Lord, this isn't fair...

For the rest of the day, he didn't stop praying, though perhaps it sounded more like a tirade from his sore heart straight to God. Even then, the demand of his spirit to *do* something didn't slacken.

If he had thought of Sadie Allen much before, it was nothing compared to now. She and Reid consumed his thoughts. Even when he returned to base and resumed his work in the control tower, he found it near impossible to set them aside. Which was problematic, as his job demanded his full attention.

A week after their reunion, exhausted from lack of sleep and stressed from the combination of a demanding job and worry about Sadie, Connor knew he couldn't let it go.

Even still, he had no idea what he could do.

Chapter Five

(in which memories are hard)

Connor Murphy invaded her thoughts for more than a week.

Along with the intrusion of the concerned look in his eyes and the gentle way he'd cradled her when she'd burst into tears, was the far less lovely memories of things long since passed. Memories she'd spent too many years attempting to drown by any means she'd been able to conceive.

For all of her destructive methods, those moments that were sealed in the recesses of Sugar Pine history remained stubbornly active in her mind. She could not escape. After a week of interrupted sleep and evasive peace, Sadie decided it was time to reckon with her seventeen-year-old self.

The hike from the dirt road to the beaver lodge was more of a walk than anything, but getting past the falls on the much more challenging trail would require determination now that her energy levels had tanked. Still, Sadie pushed up the narrow path, after having taken a ten-minute reprieve in the quietness of the meadow, allowing the bright sun of the new year to soak into her achy bones. Walking helped relieve some of the pain in her back, though it never really went away, but the activity taxed her stamina.

The two inches of snowpack on the trail crunched under her boots as she made the final push up the incline that would put her on the more level place of much of her past recreation. Everyone in Sugar Pine knew where the best sledding hill was, and conveniently there was a small pond that would reliably freeze solid enough in the winter for shoe skating. They'd spend hours there—usually just the teenage crowd, though sometimes a family with younger children would make the trek up to enjoy a day of winter play.

Three steps past the leveling point, Sadie paused to let her heart rate settle and her heavy puffing ease. As she caught her breath, she scanned the view. The gentle slope across the clearing glistened with bluish-white invitation in the gleam of the cloudless day. At its base, the ice of the pond shone a smooth, dullish white, and at its edges, snow gathered like puffy pillows. Evergreens rimmed the clearing, the perfect dark contrast to soften the stark winter palette.

The beauty pressed against her in a haunting way, and her pulse that was already too fast spiked again. Why had she come here again?

For reckoning. She squeezed her eyes shut. *God help me.* And then she looked again, allowing former scenes their demanded replay against the emptiness of the setting, forcing herself to watch them again.

Ivy Levens had been one of those girls—the kind everyone adored because she was everything desirable. From their first encounter in kindergarten, Sadie had liked Ivy. The girl with silky black hair and sparkling blue eyes had been nice to her, and goodness knew, Sadie needed a kind soul that day. She'd arrived at school and then stood in her appointed line, quiet tears trickling down her face.

"I'll pray for you the whole day, Sadie," Mom had said, a hitch in her voice. "And I promise I'll be right here to pick you up when school's out."

Her mom's offered comfort didn't help at all. Why did Sadie have to go to school? Mom had taught letters and numbers to her, and at almost six, Sadie could read simple words. Surely Mom could keep teaching her, couldn't she?

Sadie had been a painfully shy girl and a homebody. She liked playing quietly with her stuffed panda named Norman, baking cookies with her mom, and hearing Dad read out his latest rough draft for his next sermon. Whoever determined school to be necessary? Not anyone who understood Sadie's timid heart. It seemed cruel.

But Mom insisted. So there Sadie stood, trying her very best to be a good girl but unable to stop her tears from leaking.

"Hi." The girl with the black hair cozied up next to her, a look of sympathy and kindness on her face. "Are you okay?"

Sadie sniffed and nodded.

The girl took her hand—the one Mom wasn't holding. "Don't worry. See, we're in the same class." She pointed to the line they were both in. "I'll be with you."

"I don't know you," Sadie stammered.

"I'm Ivy."

"Oh."

"Ivy Levens. What's your name?"

"Sadie Allen."

"See? Now we know each other, and we can be friends."

And so they were. From that moment in their very young lives all the way through school, until their senior year, Sadie and Ivy had been best friends.

Though, Ivy was everyone's friend, it seemed. She was the kind of girl who was loved wherever she went. Not only was she outgoing and kind, Ivy Levens was beautiful. Stunningly beautiful. And smart. Unbelievably smart. She was perfect.

Sadie had to own some jealousy from time to time when it came to Ivy, but usually it was mild enough to laugh away. Nothing that would cause their friendship harm. Nothing that would be toxic to Sadie's life.

Not until Connor Murphy asked the most probable candidate for homecoming queen to be his date for the dance. No, more specifically, not until Ivy accepted Connor's request. That was when Sadie's mild dose of jealously mushroomed to toxic levels, particularly since Ivy had known since they'd been fourteen that Sadie had an unquenchable crush on the tall green-eyed Murphy boy.

Toxic envy coursing through a heart already unsteady from a deep sense of inferiority was a sure recipe for destruction.

The friendship was lost. Sadie convinced herself it was Ivy's fault, and likely for the better. Who really wanted to live in the shadow cast by the most perfect girl God ever created anyway?

And actually, Ivy wasn't nearly as perfect as everyone thought.

She broke curfew sometimes and snuck into her room through the window when she did. Also, when it was only Sadie and Ivy together, Ivy would use words that would have shocked both their parents. And once when Ivy didn't study for a chemistry test like she should have—because she'd snuck out with a boy whom her parents had said she couldn't date—Ivy had cheated, because she needed to maintain her 4.0.

Connor didn't know the real Ivy. The sneaky, cheating, back-stabbing Ivy Levens that Sadie knew.

As the weeks passed and Connor and Ivy became the royal couple of Sugar Pine High, bitterness seethed through Sadie's heart and mind. But she kept it buckled in. No one knew how Sadie had come to hate Ivy. Least of all, Connor.

Christmas came and went. Connor bought Ivy a necklace—one with a tiny diamond that sparkled inside the silver heart. Everyone said he'd buy her a ring next. But then, after the holiday break, something happened.

Ivy broke up with Connor, shocking everyone in school. Their very own *High School Musical* couple had fallen apart—how could anyone ever hope for happily ever after if those two couldn't find it? In the middle of all the drama and speculation, Sadie saw her chance.

Connor was in her English class—the one Ivy wasn't in because Miss Too-Good-for-Everyone was in the AP class. That new semester, Connor and Sadie had been assigned to the same study group. Sadie had a legitimate reason to talk to him every day. Then they swapped numbers and started texting. First, about class.

Did you remember to study for the vocab test?

Oh yeah! He'd reply. *Thanks—saved me!*

I saw you at the end of school...you were wearing a frowny face.

Yeah...just trying to deal.

Because of Ivy?

Yeah. Guess everyone knows.

Why'd you break up?

She did. Said we needed to take a big step back.

Why?

Reasons.

You know you're too good for her, right?

LOL...thanks for trying to make me feel better. But we both know she's galaxies better than me.

Not true. She can be really sneaky.

What?

Connor, I'm sure you only saw the best of Ivy, but take if from the girl who used to be her best friend. She's a hypocrite. If she made you feel like you weren't good enough, then she's even worse than a hypocrite.

Those texts, written over the span of a couple of weeks, seemed to have changed how Connor saw Sadie. He smiled at her more at school. Walked with her through the halls. Met her at her locker. And texted her at night.

When the winter dance came around at the end of January, Sadie's teenage dream finally came true. Connor Murphy asked her to be his date.

Her. Sadie Allen. Not perfect Ivy Levens. Sadie pretended that she didn't even feel bad for the things she'd said about her former friend. After all, all was fair in love and war.

Back in the present, standing near the pond, a shiver tumbled through Sadie, jarring her away from the memories. She blinked into the brightness of the sun as the empty space refocused into the reality of the moment. The cold hardness of her heart toward her friend made her tremble again. Sadie had coddled the feeling back then, feeding it with thoughts of Ivy's betrayal—some real, but most imagined.

With her mittened hand, Sadie palmed her chest and rubbed. Remembering herself back then was physically painful. Desperate to turn away, to switch off the replay, and to trek back to the warm safety of her parents' home and the comfortable distraction Reid was certain to provide, Sadie almost yielded. But then, there would be the nighttime. Always, there were the long, quiet hours of the night, when she yearned for sleep to ease the ache of her tired body but often found only bits and pieces of reprieve as these memories refused to be put down.

Reckon with them.

That was why she'd pushed herself into this hike. Against the twinge in her back and the instinct to turn away from something she knew would be painful, Sadie forced her strides toward the edge of the pond. There, she scanned the empty scene and let the old things come back...

Connor had been the perfect gentleman at the dance. From the flowers he'd brought her, to the dinner they'd shared, and then the dance...

Everything had been the stuff of her dreams—and the best part? She, plain old shy Sadie Allen, owned Connor's complete attention the entire night. He danced with no one else. Stayed by her side. Held her hand as he worked around the room to chat it up with a few of his basketball buddies. Bragged about her on occasion. *Sadie's super smart. She's the reason I'm acing English. Doesn't she look gorgeous tonight?*

At some point as the evening drew to a close, however, Sadie caught on. Connor was working really hard at *not* looking at Ivy while at the same time he'd perfectly timed his compliments about Sadie and the moments he swept her into his arms and out onto the floor, to be moments when his ex was in close proximity.

When he dropped Sadie off at her house that night, Sadie invited him in to watch a movie.

"Nah, I think I'm gonna pass." He'd pushed his hand through his hair and glanced away. "We've got a couple of games this week, you know, and there's church tomorrow. Just want to make sure I don't start off the week exhausted."

And then Sadie had understood. Connor's attention had been entirely calculated. He was trying win Ivy back by making her jealous.

That night Sadie waded through her battling emotions. She was so angry at Connor for using her. And still angry at Ivy for stealing the boy Sadie had been dreaming of for years. And yet...and yet there was that part of her heart that had feasted on envy, and now on anger. That corner of her heart connived a plan for her victory.

She'd play along with Connor's ploy, take advantage of every moment he used her and make sure they were moments he never forgot. Throughout the following week, whenever he sought her out, she made sure he had her undivided attention. She went to his games, waited for him to change afterward, and when he took her hand—after he'd subtly checked the cheerleading line to confirm that Ivy was still there—Sadie fit herself snugly at his side. On Saturday afternoon when he texted to see if she wanted to go up to the sledding hill, she knew there would be a group in company—Ivy among them.

But Sadie went. And when Connor pulled her onto the frozen pond to shoe skate, she moved along with him. He scanned the scene at her back as they slipped and slid in an awkward, seemingly romantic dance, and then his attention lowered on her. And she knew.

Ivy, her black hair stunning beneath her cream snow hat that also made her sapphire eyes nearly glow, was watching.

Connor paused, a flash of uncertainty in his lowered gaze, as if he knew exactly what he was doing and knew for certain it was wrong. But Sadie convinced herself that the indecision she'd glimpsed in that moment was his affections shifting from Ivy to her, and she wasn't about to let that moment pass. Already in the cove of his arms, Sadie slipped her hands over his coat, from his shoulders to the unzipped collar, and tugged. As she stretched on her toes, his mouth lowered to hers.

The kiss, to be honest, was a disappointing first kiss. Chilled and lifeless—just his dead lips meeting hers and holding sufficiently long to make a scene. But it was enough to make Ivy Levens leave the sledding hill. Crying.

Seventeen-year-old Sadie had batted away the stab of guilt that threatened to fill her as she'd held on to Connor's hand, even while knowing he wanted to go after Ivy. He didn't dare though. Not after he'd kissed Sadie. Instead he'd stood stiff as an ice statue at her side, watching as Ivy disappeared down the trail and through the sugar pine trees. His glance at Sadie was pure regret, and the agony of his reaction was like being plowed over by an avalanche. That alone was enough to shake Sadie to her battered core.

But it didn't end there.

Neither Connor nor Sadie had banked on the events that played out beyond their little charade that afternoon. They'd never imagined that would be the last time anyone saw Ivy Levens alive.

***

Connor stared at the ceiling through the gray shadows. His alarm wouldn't sound for at least another thirty minutes, but he'd been awake for over an hour. He should have gotten up, gone to the fitness center, and pushed himself into a workout that would silence the thoughts robbing his rest. But something kept him from taking that evasive course—and not just physical and mental exhaustion. It was like there was a demand on him to hear what wouldn't let him be. To remember. To repent.

And then to act.

Honestly, that demand didn't make sense to him. While he knew he'd never be able to forget the tangled mess he'd woven between Ivy, Sadie, and himself, he had repented. He understood that God's forgiveness had met his remorse, removing his guilt—at least for life in eternity. But this requirement that he think on the past seemed divine, and Connor couldn't reconcile it.

Even still, he wasn't willing to ignore it.

Previous to seeing Sadie again, his prayers had been focused on her—her heart's healing, her stability and happiness. Especially since she'd been sent to a recovery center for at-risk young women. In little Sugar Pine, Sadie's attempted suicide wasn't a secret. Her dad, who had pastored their church for years, had stepped down from the pulpit. Her mom, who had been as social as a barn swallow, had withdrawn. Why they hadn't left Sugar Pine was never clear, but the reason they'd sent Sadie away was.

She needed help, and Mr. and Mrs. Allen had been afraid what they could offer was insufficient. More, they felt that keeping Sadie in Sugar Pine, where so much trauma had buried their daughter, wasn't helpful.

Connor ached to know that Sadie's path had only taken harder turns. She hadn't said much about Reid's dad, but enough for

Connor to gather that whoever the man was, he wasn't a good one. And she'd said Connor didn't really want to know the details of her life after Sugar Pine.

Thing was, as Connor sifted through old memories and new revelations there in the predawn moments, he felt strongly that he needed to know—if not those details she wanted to keep concealed, then at least what was happening with her now.

There.

Connor sat up as purpose locked in his mind. Right there was it. The action he was compelled toward wasn't about the past—as regretful as he was for it. It was about the present—and the future. Sadie's future.

Planting his feet firmly on the chilly floor of his lonely room, Connor sucked in a breath of cold air, exhaled, and then anchored his elbows to his knees, bowing his head to pray.

I'm willing, Lord. Show me what—and how.

Chapter Six

(in which Sadie goes to the doctor)

Sadie snipped the final bits of wispy stray hair from Reid's neck. The first time she'd trimmed his fine baby hair, she'd cried. That had been two years ago, though, and now she simply brushed the yellowish-white clippings from his back and then fluffed the top of his head with her forked fingers.

"No more mop head," she said.

Reid giggled. "I don't have a mop head."

"Not anymore." She came around in front of him and cupped his chin to tip his face. "What do you say to your mommy?"

"Thanks, Mama, 'cept I didn't even think I needed a haircut, 'cuz there was no mop on my head."

Dad stood up from his place at the table across the room and walked toward her and Reid. "Definitely didn't have the clean military cut Connor wears."

While Reid's eyes rounded, Sadie wrestled with the uncomfortable curling in her stomach. Why would Dad even bring Connor up?

"Mr. Sergeant Connor has short hair, doesn't he!"

And then, at her son's response, Sadie understood Dad's aim. The boy had been enamored with Connor, possessing the man's afternoon with games of dominos, the card game war, and begging for more stories of Connor working in the tower watching the jets come in. Maybe if Sadie had taken advantage of her son's obvious adoration of Mr. Sergeant Connor *before* she'd sat Reid onto a stool, her scissors in hand, and told him he needed a trim, the kid wouldn't have gone mopey on her.

"He does. Always did too." Dad winked at Sadie and then patted Reid's head. "Always looked sharp, like my grandson does now."

Reid felt the top of his head, and then his face scrunched. "Maybe you need to cut more off, Mom. Like Mr. Sergeant Connor."

Great. One extreme to the other. She eyed Dad, who shrugged and chuckled.

"Can't today, buddy. We have to head out soon." Sadie wiped her good trimming scissors on her soft cloth and put them away, then moved toward the hall closet to retrieve the broom.

"I don't mind if Reid stays with me, Sadie. We can hang out here, just the guys."

Dad's offer stirred a mixture of warmth and dread in her heart. "I know. Thanks. But Mom will keep track of him while I'm with the doctor." She stopped sweeping and stood up to meet Dad's gaze. "I just feel like I need to have him with me."

With a hand that was at once meaty and shriveled with age, one that shook as he reached, Dad touched the side of her face. "Then we'll all go," he whispered.

Sadie blinked at the burn in her eyes and nodded. "Thank you."

Fighting hard to regrip her composure, Sadie finished the job of cleaning up and then went to her room to change. They would have nearly a two-hour drive to the specialty clinic—one that she likely would have to make on a regular basis, depending on the action plan her new doctor would recommend. She chose something comfortable to wear, a pair of loose-fitting jeans and an ombre sweater on which the color faded from top to bottom, from midnight blue to the softest shade of emerald green. As she twisted her long hair—now much thinner than it had been even a year before—into a simple braid that would fall on her back, her phone let her know that someone had texted her.

Likely a reminder from the clinic. As if one could forget such an appointment.

The number flashed above the text without a name—and the prefix wasn't local. But the content caught her breath, and she lowered onto her bed, one palm against her throbbing heart, as she read.

Sadie...I keep thinking about you. I feel like we need to meet again. Would you be willing to do that?

She stared at the screen, feeling her scowl deepen as she reread the message. Unsure if she should be flattered or freaked out, she debated about answering at all. Finally she typed out a response.

Who is this?

Then she gripped her phone. She shouldn't have responded. Whoever it was now knew for sure that they'd reached her. What if Reid's dad was looking for them?

Too late, buddy, she thought. *You surrendered your rights.*

Her phone vibrated against her palm.

Connor. Sorry. I didn't think about you not knowing. I got your number from your dad.

Connor? An ache filled the place that had just panicked with fear. Connor Murphy had been thinking about her? Why?

Because he still felt guilty. Their face-to-face reconciliation hadn't been enough for him. She'd looked him in those forest-green eyes and assured him of her forgiveness. But she got it—these past years had been gnarled with regret for her too.

That's sweet of you to think of me, Connor. I meant it when I told you that I've forgiven you. You don't owe me anything. I promise.

He needed to release. How well she knew...they both needed to let the past go. So much easier said than done.

I believed you. But I still feel like there are things between us not settled. Like there was a reason you came home when I was there on leave—a reason I saw you. I really think we need to get together again, if you're okay with that?

The strumming of her pulse still moved with a bold rhythm, but at that text, a gentle warmth moved through her veins. Ah, she was still that girl at heart. The one who was likely to swoon at any kindness offered from the likes of Connor Murphy. The one who would take advantage of his weak moments.

Was this a weak moment for him? Was it weak to seek

restoration?

Sadie had been one to run. She'd run hard into the dark and hoped the people she'd left behind would never catch up. *That* had been weakness. This, from Connor, this was his dignity and honor at work.

Don't you have to stay on base or something? She sifted through the vestiges of excuses even while she warmed to the idea of seeing him again. Maybe with Reid. Her son would be all wonder and smiles if he could see Mr. Sergeant Connor Murphy again. Heaven knew her boy needed honorable men in his life.

I do have time off on occasion. I could take another day of leave.

So he was serious, and the growing part of her latching on to the idea of seeing him again—particularly for Reid sake—overtook the dwindling doubt.

I'm actually heading down the hills today, toward the base.

Serious?

Yes. That clinic appointment I told you about is your direction.

What time?

Is my appointment? I don't want you to be there for that. Pretty direct, she knew, but after her life had collapsed due in large part to lies and deception, Sadie had resolved to become a straight shooter.

I respect that. His immediate respect of her wishes made her remember one of the reasons she'd liked him so much when they were kids. Connor had always been respectful.

Her phone rattled in her palm again. *But could I meet you after?*

Yes. If you have time and know of a place. But you should know that Reid and my parents will be with me.

I know a place. There's a park with a trail that follows a creek.

That sounds lovely. She reached for that determination to be honest again. *But I doubt I'll be up to doing much by then.*

Of course. Maybe I could take Reid on a miniature hike? There's a bridge that goes over the river, and I usually see wildlife. He liked the beaver dam so much. And you could maybe process or rest for a bit with you parents. Would that be helpful?

And there her heart melted. Sadie shut her eyes and indulged in a moment of aching what if. Connor was a good man—what girl wouldn't sigh just a little at the thoughtfulness of a good man? With a long breath, she brushed aside the yearning that had just bloomed in a back corner of her heart. Though still a woman with a beating heart, she was aware now that she had a responsibility to guard it. For herself and for others' sake. *Mostly for his.*

Yes. Mostly for Connor's sake, because that honor-driven sense of duty could, in fact, be a weakness in him.

***

That's thoughtful of you, Connor. We'll meet you there. Thanks.

Connor stared at the screen, the words she'd sent him earlier that day as familiar to him now as the alphabet. He wasn't sure what he was looking for as he studied those few simple sentences. Maybe for direction?

He gripped the phone and then crossed his arms over the steering wheel. He'd sent Sadie a pin for her to put into her GPS, and last he'd heard, she and her family were coming. Nerves squeezed his insides, though he wasn't sure why. In fact, he still wasn't sure why he was compelled to do this. He had no agenda—no plan for what to say or do with either Sadie or her parents, which made everything about waiting for whatever was to come next terribly awkward. Bending forward, Connor leaned his head against his arms.

God, what am I doing?

Reid's dark-brown eyes passed through his mind. So serious, but still little boy. One without a father...

Man, that thought was...disruptive. And persistent.

The sound of tires popping against the gravel parking lot pulled Connor out of his thoughts and his head off his arms. A dark-gray minivan drove behind him and then pulled up beside his old Pathfinder. With a glance, he found Mr. Allen in the driver's seat, and the man waved when their gazes connected. He seemed relaxed as he eased out of his vehicle, maybe even a hint of pride or respect as he smiled at Connor.

Connor exited his own car and came around to meet the Allens at the front of their vehicle. He gave Mr. Allen's outstretched hand a shake.

"Good to see you again, sir."

He chuckled. "Good to be seen." With a move toward a picnic table, he gestured toward the park. "This is a good spot."

A carpet of green spread out in front of them, even in its January state, but the scattered trees were without their leaves. A small gazebo was nearby, and in the distance, a metal bridge spanned the river that ribboned through the park, the current filling the air with a soothing backdrop of gently flowing water.

"It is." He came there often—the proximity to his housing made it convenient, and he liked the peace that hovered over the trail, especially when he walked past the picnic tables and mowed grass and deeper into the less groomed path. It had become a favorite thinking space, praying space, breathing space.

It stuck him in that moment that it was odd that this personal sanctuary was the first place he'd thought of to meet with Sadie again.

When his thoughts refocused on her, Connor stepped around the front of the van and found her at the slider door, waiting while Reid scrambled out of his seat.

"Hi, Mr. Sergeant Connor!" Reid hit the ground with both feet, stood tall, and held a salute.

The movement in his chest was warm and profound as Connor took in those brown eyes, all adoration and excitement, aimed straight at him. "Hey, buddy. No salute necessary, remember?" He knelt with a fist held forward for a bump.

Reid tapped Connor's knuckles with his and made an explosion sound. "Mom says you're gonna take me on an exploration."

"We could do that." Connor looked up at Sadie, finding her blue eyes shifting from her son to himself. He stood, and the tug he'd felt to see her again pulled harder now that she was in front of him. The pull was pain and need and...desire. All of it growing as he took in the emotion in her gaze. She was tired but grateful to him—he could see that without her saying a word. He could also make out that her visit with her doctor had not produced encouraging news.

"Hi," she breathed.

"Hey." As if they'd never been strangers, never had a complicated past between them, Connor reached for her shoulder, and she stepped to him willingly. His hand slid over her back, and he tucked her into a one-armed embrace. "Didn't go well, did it?"

Her forehead tipped against him, and she shook her head. He felt the long draw of her breath and knew she was fighting for control.

"I'm sorry, Sadie," he whispered. "What can I do?"

After a shaky exhale, she stepped away. "Just take Reid for a little bit? I haven't told my parents yet."

"They don't know?"

"They know about the cancer. Just not..." She blinked and looked toward the river.

"Okay." Connor drifted his hand over her arm to her hand and then squeezed. "How long do you need?"

Her shrug looked hopeless, making his heart crack. With pressed lips, Sadie winced and then swiped at a tear before it could trickle onto her nose. "Just a little bit."

"You got it." Finding it hard to not haul her in close and tell her it would all be okay—a promise he had absolutely no way of keeping—Connor forced his attention back to Reid, who had scampered off toward Sadie's parents, who had discreetly wandered toward a picnic table near the river. Mrs. Allen had carried a picnic basket, and Mr. Allen a cooler his wife had handed to him. Willing discipline into the desire to hold her close, Connor moved in the direction of the picnic table, leaving Sadie to compose herself.

"Hey, Reid!" When the towhead turned, all wide-eyed enthusiasm, Connor jogged to catch up. "Ready to explore?"

Reid nodded and reached a hand up. The moment that little palm slid into Connor's was the moment his heart slipped away.

One day Connor would look back on that moment. Because it changed everything.

Chapter Seven

(in which Connor has a clear calling)

Sadie lay on her back, the thick quilt covering her warm and heavy. It smelled like peppermint—like her mom. She wondered if Reid would ever associate a scent with her, if that smell would trigger this sense of love and a montage of sweet memories shared between them. Was it wrong for her to hope so?

At her sentimental wonderings, a fresh crop of silent tears rolled down the sides of her face, pooling in her hair and her pillow near her ears. So many tears that day. It'd been a hard one.

Against her shut eyelids, she saw the faces of both of her aging parents as they'd been that afternoon. It had seemed like such a contradiction—the weather had been perfectly lovely. The sun had gently worked warmth into the chilly January air, and the setting of the park was nothing but beautiful peace. Not the setting one would picture for what had transpired.

"It's not good." She'd managed to push the words around the mass in her tight throat after Connor had Reid safely on the other side of the metal bridge spanning the river. Connor looked back at her in that moment, and something in the way his gaze settled on her gave her a fresh boost of strength—enough to get the rest out. "The doctor confirmed what the clinic in Nevada had said. The cancer has spread."

Mom broke first. Her silent cries were the most heartbreaking thing for Sadie to watch, and she couldn't hold it together anymore. With his bulky arms, Dad wrapped first Mom in one arm and then pulled Sadie into the other, and they wept.

"Daddy," Sadie stuttered between sobs. "How could God do this?"

Against her own head, she felt him only shake his. There

wasn't a real answer to that hopeless question anyway. Some queries were simply empty—even if God was obligated to answer them, which He wasn't, the answer would likely not satisfy what was really needed.

The real question was, how would God see them through it?

Great is Thy faithfulness, oh God my Father...

Lying in bed, alone and feeling hopeless, she could hear Daddy's rich baritone voice in her mind. He'd sung those timeless lyrics hundreds of times, clinging to the words as if a lifeline from heaven. Never had she been so desperate to grip that salvation herself.

Sadie turned her agony to a plea. *Please see us through this. See my parents and my son... Oh Lord! My son...*

She couldn't even think the words, but her prayer lifted upward. Her last discernable thought, before exhaustion swept her into the darkness, held her in a strange place of peace within the storm.

You are the God who sees, and You are still King.

***

"Will you re-up your contract this spring?"

Connor looked at the officer across the desk, who'd been giving Connor's annual evaluation. He turned to stare out the window of the private office, his mind suddenly cluttered with thoughts that had very little to do with the air force or the excellent report he'd just been given.

"Sergeant Murphy?"

"Sir, I'm sorry." With a sharp redirection of his focus, he looked back at his superior.

"You haven't thought about it?"

"I have, sir. I mean, I had. But..." But what? All he could see in his mind right then were a pair of wide brown eyes looking up at him. All he could feel was a needy pain that involved a longing not only for that little boy but for his hurting mother. He'd spent nearly nine years as an enlisted airman, and up until the most recent Christmas, he'd had no inclination to change that status.

"We could look into OTC for you, if you're interested in

moving out of NCO. You'd be a good candidate."

"No." He'd never been interested in a higher rank. The job he'd trained for—air traffic control—was stressful enough as it was. He really didn't want the pressure and added responsibility that came with being a commissioned officer in charge of and responsible for more men and women than he already was.

Failing people and responsibilities was too heavy a burden—and Connor already wore more weight in that department than he could honestly carry. Enlisting had been an intentional move for him. He'd wanted to serve his country and the people he loved without risking another life catastrophe.

The officer across the desk held him with a curious study. "Sergeant Murphy, you excel at what you do. I have no doubt you would make an excellent commissioned officer, and every evaluation on your record proves that you have what it takes to make it through OTC and beyond."

"Thank you, sir."

"But still no?"

"Yes, sir."

"Did you not intend to be a career man?"

"I did, sir."

"As enlisted?"

"Yes, sir."

"So you'll renew your contract?"

"I..." Connor pressed his lips and tried to unjumble his thoughts.

When he didn't answer right away, his commanding officer stood. "It's all right, Murphy. You don't need to answer right now anyway. I'm just surprised."

He wasn't the only one. Well, maybe confused was a more apt description for Connor.

After being dismissed, he strode out of the office building and toward the parking lot. He'd chosen to live off base on this assignment—and he hadn't even been sure why. Every other move, he'd lived on base. He had a short drive ahead of him, and his thoughts tumbled recklessly as his body shifted into autopilot.

He'd adjusted to military life. The demand on his time—whether he was working or not. The demand on his personal appearance and how he carried himself at all times. The demand on his social life—understanding the social rules that existed within the ranks. The knowing that ultimately he was at the air force's bidding. A PCS could be just around the corner. A required class for new certification or recertification could be the next new demand on his nonworking hours. His life was not his own, which had been fine. Connor had liked the knowledge that while he might not know what was coming around the next bend, there was direction in it, and he wouldn't have to necessarily figure it out. Just adapt.

But there was a new bend in his life, one entirely unexpected. Unexplained, for that matter. Because sitting in that office, wondering about re-upping his contract, all he'd been able to think about was what would happen to Sadie and Reid.

And wondering why that question felt so important.

Sadie couldn't do military life—not being sick as she was. He had no question about that, and frankly he wouldn't want that for her anyway. And Reid...

Why were these thoughts even in his head?

As the apartment complex he'd claimed as home for the past two years came into view, a feeling—so strong it was nearly tangible—swept through him. It was memory—one made very recently—and a direction. A calling.

He parked his car, moved from the vehicle to the stairs that would take him to his third-story dwelling, and began to climb. As he moved, Connor closed his right hand. The sensation of a little boy's fingers in his grip lingered there.

The calling focused into perfect clarity. Reid needed a father.

***

How are you today?

Sadie rested in her dad's leather recliner near the fire while Reid and Pops put together a Lego set—one Reid had opened on Christmas morning. They worked together with quiet companionship, Pops often asking Reid what was next, and Reid carefully studying the pictures in the instruction booklet in his serious little boy way. The text from Connor came unexpectedly, yet somehow Sadie was not surprised.

She'd thought of him often over the past few days since they'd met at the park. Wondered, when she made her morning tea and watched the sunrise, if he'd started his day yet. Hoped, when she changed into her warm jammies at the close of a day, that his had been good—not too stressful as he carried the responsibilities of an air traffic controller on a military base.

We are better today. Adjusting, she typed back.

Her heart moved with a warm squeeze as she sent her response to him. Why did he continue to treat her with so much kindness? He wasn't obligated...

No, but he *felt* obligated.

Sadie didn't like the painful stab of that thought. It had been so much nicer to simply think that Connor's thoughtfulness toward her came from something more than guilt-induced duty.

I have a couple days off. Thought I'd drive up to Sugar Pine.

The tension between wanting his attention to be sincere and knowing Connor was acting out of regret pulled even more. Sadie didn't know what to do with what he was saying and doing.

I'm sure your mom will like that.

His response was immediate. *I want to see you.*

With a rush of heat running over her face, and a stifled sigh, Sadie squeezed her eyes shut. *Lord, what do I do with this?*

Her phone vibrated against her palm. *Can I see you again?*

Why did he have to be so...so classic Connor Murphy. Sadie wanted to burst into tears. Connor had always been quietly determined, and save for one brief period of time, she'd known him always to be kind. To everyone. But this attention was so personal, so forward. So heartbreakingly...

Special.

Sadie had spent a lot of years not being okay and fighting against her own inadequacies. It'd taken a lot of arrogant mistakes that took her deeper and deeper into depression and a lifestyle that was, frankly, dangerous, before she'd finally come to a life-changing conclusion: she couldn't make the pain go away.

She was never going to save herself from herself.

It was there, when Reid had been a baby and Sadie could no longer pretend that she was sufficient for her own needs, let alone her infant son's, that she finally understood the heart of the man, in Jesus's story, who'd beaten his chest with a broken spirit and said, "Oh God, be merciful to me! For I am a sinner!"

Sadie couldn't escape her mistakes. She would never drown them with a life that screamed *independent and fierce*. The guilt refused to be appeased with dark nights of self-loathing, nor could she escape the shame by stuffing herself with mantras meant to elevate her own esteem.

She'd been caught under the weight of bad choices. Of sin. Only God's mercy could lift that burden. Only His forgiveness could remove the guilt of her shame. In that moment, nearly four years ago, with her ugly, broken, helpless heart laid bare before God, she'd been that person in Jesus's story. Begging for His mercy because she was a sinner.

Life had changed from that point—her spirit felt new. Though she still struggled with regret and carried the consequences of her life choices, she no longer felt like she would drown in her own guilt. She'd become a woman living in God's great mercy.

Connor didn't know all of this. If he did, would he find the same freedom? So much of her leapt at the hope of it for him—Sadie didn't want him living under this weight of duty and penitent obligation for the rest of his life. But as she thought of the way he'd been her help and support in recent days, she sure did have a longing for something else. One that had been there since she'd been a smitten fourteen-year-old.

Sadie? There was that persistence delivered in his text.

Why did he have to focus his attention and kindness on her now, when she was truly needy and oh-so vulnerable? What was the right thing to do?

Only if you truly want to, she answered.

I do.

Again, Sadie gripped her phone and thought carefully before

she typed. *Connor, we've talked about this already, but I feel like I need to say it again. I forgive you. Maybe you need to forgive me? Because the thing is, I knew what you were doing that day on the ice—I knew exactly why you kissed me. It was me who took advantage. I thought that somehow if I played the charade with you that you'd suddenly see me. Want me. It was every bit as selfish of me to do what I did as it was for you.*

Her hands shook after she sent that last text, and the long minutes after were filled with a taut strumming of her pulse. Finally, after she'd concluded that Connor wasn't going to respond, one last text lit her screen.

We'll talk this weekend. About everything.

Chapter Eight
(in which Connor and Sadie talk about everything)

Sitting in his car with the engine turned off in the Allens' driveway, Connor reread her last text for at least the twentieth time. Clearly Sadie didn't want him to live with a guilty conscience, which was generous of her. It also confused him. Why had she kept away from Sugar Pine all these years if she'd felt that way? If she didn't want him to live in guilt, why did she feel like she had to take up permanent residence in the trenches of shame?

The contradiction stirred frustration in him, the kind that provoked a touch of anger. Or maybe he was angry at the circumstances. Why would God allow a twenty-seven-year-old single mom to get cancer?

Emotion was overriding his thinking. That was the problem, and he hadn't allowed that particular issue to grip him in years. Not since Ivy. Giving emotion lead over logic and clear thinking was dangerous, and he and Sadie both wore heart scars to prove it.

Connor squeezed the steering wheel of his parked car, inhaled a calming breath, and squeezed his eyes shut.

Father, this feels precarious. I don't really know what I'm doing. All I know is I'm supposed to be here. Show me Your path. I could really use Your wisdom.

The prayer felt right, even if he still didn't own confidence. The words *humble trust* settled into his mind, calming the anxiety that had brewed moments before. He climbed out of his car and the stepped up the deck to the Allens' front door.

Reid answered his knock. "Mr. Sergeant Connor!"

The boy's enthusiastic greeting made Connor grin, and so did Reid's immediate switch to a serious salute. Connor knelt. "No salute necessary, buddy. I'm just Connor."

Dark, searching eyes took him in with so much open admiration, and a claim moved in Connor's heart. One that at that moment, Connor had no legitimate reason to make, but he didn't have the resolve to temper it. Instead he reached to cup the little boy's arm. "How are you, Reid?"

"I'm good. Pops got me a log set, and we built a cabin."

It took a moment for Connor to translate a *log set*. "Ah, Lincoln Logs. They were a favorite in my house too. Did you know I have brothers?"

"No." Those brown eyes grew. "How many?"

"Six."

"Six! Wow. I don't have any brothers. Not even a sister. Just Mom and me."

A subtle ache tugged. "How is your mom today?"

Reid shrugged. "She's here. Want to say hi?"

Connor pushed to his feet. "Yeah, if that's okay."

That little hand slid into his. Amazing how such small fingers could grip his whole heart with compelling ferocity. Connor silently prayed for wisdom and direction again as he walked into the Allens' home to find Sadie.

***

Being at the upper pond and sledding hill with him was painful.

The last time they'd shared this setting, the fabric of life as they'd known it had ripped. Having Reid with them was a bit of a distraction, if not a balm. Connor tirelessly doted on her son, taking him up the sledding hill time after time, riding in tandem with Reid on the saucer disk he'd brought with them.

Sadie watched the pair with twin doses of appreciation and yearning. Reid needed such a man in his life. With a conscious effort, Sadie chose gratitude for Connor's pouring into her son, even if it was momentary.

"Hey, buddy, mind if I take a little break?" Connor lowered to one knee in the snow at the base of the hill and looked at Reid as if his young feelings mattered.

"Are you tired, Mr. Sergeant Connor?"

Chucking, Conor bobbed his head. "Been a long time since I've spent a day on this hill. But also, I wanted to talk with your mom. Are you okay with that?"

With that ever-studious expression of his, Reid looked at Sadie. Her heart melted as she smiled, then blew a kiss his way. Slowly, his solemn gaze latched back on to Connor, and he nodded.

"Thanks, buddy."

"I can still sled, right?"

"Think so—if you stay on the path we cut."

"And you'll watch?"

"You bet."

"You won't leave?"

Connor winced.

Reid's question stabbed Sadie's heart as well. Perhaps this attention Connor was giving Reid wasn't a good idea. Not when it was temporary. The last thing she wanted for Reid was more change, more grief.

"Not until later," Connor answered Reid's question. "Not until all the sledding is done."

Again, Reid nodded. Then he turned to scramble up the hill, the disk sled bouncing against the snow behind him.

With her attention still on her little boy, Sadie felt more than watched Connor approach. When he stopped at the edge of the water-proof quilt he'd brought for her to sit on, she finally turned her gaze to him.

Goodness, the man was handsome. In looks, for sure, Connor had always been attractive. But now, as she'd watched him with Reid...wow. Sadie sat a little breathless as he lowered next to her, a half grin forming on those firm lips. His gaze lingered on her, and she warmed at the feeling that he was taking her in slowly, purposefully.

"You doing okay?" he asked.

Heat crawling against the chill of her cheeks, Sadie nodded.

Then she adjusted her hat and redirected her attention to Reid. He was nearly to the top of the hill, and when he reached it, he turned around with a wave.

"He's a lot like you," Connor said.

Sadie snorted a laugh as she waved back to Reid. "He looks nothing like me."

"I didn't say that—although I think he has your nose. I said he *is* a lot like you. Quiet. A little bit serious. Always taking everything in."

She peeked at Connor, finding his eyes steady on her. "You noticed this?"

"Yeah, I did—I do. Then and now."

Not knowing what to say, Sadie pressed her lips together and nodded. At the top of the hill, Reid situated himself onto the disc and called, "Ready?"

Sadie gave him a thumbs-up, and Connor yelled, "Clear for takeoff!"

Her serious four-year-old son laughed as he flew down the hill, and Sadie tucked the moment into her heart as a treasure. This day had been a treasure, thanks to the man at her side.

"Thank you for this," she said, finding Connor's eyes again. "For being so good to Reid. And me."

He nodded, his grin fading as he turned his attention from the boy on the hill back to her. "Can we go back to your text the other day?"

Looking to her mittened hands, a sense of foreboding tightened her stomach. She felt Connor's unwavering stare on her, and her heart throbbed. "What...what did I say?"

He didn't hesitate. "That I needed to forgive you."

Suddenly the chill of this winter's day seeped in deeper, and she felt trapped.

"Sadie, as far as I'm concerned, that day, that whole situation was my fault."

Drawing a breath, she shook her head. "You don't understand. I knew what you were doing, that you were trying to make Ivy jealous so that she'd rethink breaking up with you. I wasn't ignorant or—"

"You said. But I—"

"Listen." She pinned her look on him. "*I* was trying to hurt her. *I* was jealous, and I had been jealous of Ivy for a long time. When you started dating her after she knew that I had a crush on you, that jealousy turned into a monster. I wanted to hurt her."

A long, miserable silence tolled between them. Hanging his head, Connor nodded.

"I know," he whispered. "I mean, I knew. And I took advantage."

Against her wish for self-control, Sadie's body shook, not from the cold but from the onslaught of those days from the past.

Connor turned so that he was facing her. "I'm sorry, Sadie."

She nodded, fighting to maintain her dignity and self-control. "You're forgiven. I keep telling you—" She reached between them and covered his knee. "Truly, Connor, live forgiven. Free. Don't spend any more time in bondage because of me. I made my own choices."

Leaning toward her, he gripped her arm. "This is why we need to talk about this. Sadie, *you* live in bondage."

She closed her mouth and looked back to the hill. Reid neared the top again, ready to take another flying trip back down. Slowly, she shook her head.

"Why have you never been back?" Connor pushed into her silence.

Waving to Reid, she ignored Connor's question. It reached too deep and pulled at things she'd thought had been at long last laid to rest. Reid started down again, his slow slide gaining momentum and his joyful laugh a stark contradiction to the turmoil swirling inside her.

"Sadie." Somewhere in the space of her not answering him, Connor had removed his glove, and now he cupped her cheek, turning her face back to his. "Why?"

The buried memories erupted, and she could no long win the fight against her long-held regret. "I said horrible things about her." Once loosed, the words tumbled out. "She was my best friend for most of my life, and I resorted to gossip and slander because I was mad. And then...then she *died*. I felt like it was my fault. How can I live in this little town, face everyone who loved her? Everyone who knows..."

"She was in a car accident. That wasn't your fault. It wasn't anyone's fault."

Sadie nodded, her emotions completely turned by the force of this confession—one not made out loud to anyone before. Hadn't she already dealt with this? God had forgiven her—why did this still feel so raw?

"I never got to apologize to her." As the answer tumbled from her lips—as much as her own realization as it was an explanation to Connor—Sadie buried her face into her mittens. "I'm sorry. I'm so sorry that I did that to a friend..."

At some point Connor's arms had surrounded her, and she was being held by this man who understood every bit of her pain. There, in the protection of his hold, Sadie wrestled with a collision of feelings yet again. His kindness and understanding felt wonderful, and yet she knew keenly her own wretchedness.

Connor's life could have looked so much different right now. If it hadn't been for her.

***

He spent the whole day with them, even enjoying supper at the Allens' table rather than his mom's—which to be honest, was likely to hurt Mom's feelings, since this was a short visit. But he felt compelled to spend the time with Sadie and Reid, and Mr. and Mrs. Allen welcomed his presence, even encouraged it. After they'd eaten and the meal was cleaned away, her parents wandered off together, leaving Sadie and Reid with Connor.

Worn out from a day in the snow, Reid brought a book to Sadie, and with a look of pure mother's love, she snuggled with him on the couch and read. Though he felt a little awkward and out of place, Connor watched the pair with a heart that continued to expand for both of them.

After *the end*, Sadie kissed Reid's hair and gave him a squeeze. "Tell Mr. Connor good night and thank you for the day of sledding."

Reid slipped off the couch and edged in front of Connor, a sudden shyness in his expression. "Thank you, Mr. Sergeant Connor." His big brown eyes fixed on Connor's face as if Reid thought he was the best thing since chocolate milk.

Man, this kid could own his heart.

"Just Connor." He brushed the tips of his fingers against the ends of Reid's short blond hair. When the boy leaned forward, Connor pulled him into a hug. "Good night, buddy."

"Night." Reid wiggled back, his look taking Connor in one more time, and then he moved quietly down the hall.

Sadie walked after him, her movement slow and looking a little pained. While Sadie tucked her son in, Connor took the few moments alone to pray. When she came back, lowering slowly onto the couch across from him, he purposefully studied her, taking in her tired eyes, her drained pallor.

"Today was too much for you, wasn't it?"

She looked at her hands. "No. Today was nice—especially for Reid. Thank you."

His chest tightened as he watched her. How could a single mom navigate such overwhelming trials? He *needed* to do something—honor demanded some kind of action.

Connor reached across the space between them and covered her hands. "What can I do?"

Her tender smile was appreciative. "It is what it is. There's nothing to do, Connor."

"Sadie, I want to help you. And Reid." He shifted from the chair beside her to the place on the cushions next to her. "Tell me how."

She chuckled a little helplessly. "You could marry me."

Her words were like the tumblers on a lock all clicking into place. His thumb moved over her thin fingers, and he became aware of how cold her hands were. Heart throbbing, he let the idea sink in deeper, finding there was already space in his heart for it to settle.

"I'm teasing." Sadie's wide blue gaze flew up to his, panic

making her eyes spark. "Connor, I'm absolutely teasing you. Please don't—"

"Reid needs a father," he murmured.

He watched her swallow hard, her small, plastered smile fading into a look of pain. "Connor, don't..." Her hand gripped his, and the pressure she squeezed against his fingers was that of desperation. "I. Was. Teasing." All laughter left her voice, leaving only the strict warning.

She didn't want him.

Could he blame her? No, not with the way they reminded each other of a past both could barely deal with on their own.

But that didn't address the truth of the matter. Reid needed a dad. Further, Sadie needed help. This fierce impression in his soul wasn't letting up—he'd been issued a divine command to care for and protect this small family.

"I think it's been a day." Sadie moved her hand from his and slid away from him as she stood.

Connor held his determined look on her.

A faint blush dusted over her pale cheeks, and she looked away. Shaking her head in an answer to his silent insistence, she stepped backward. "Good night, Connor."

He had no choice but to let her go and to show himself out. But the lock had been turned and the door opened, and his heart and mind had already stepped through.

All through the night, he replayed moments from that day. The way Reid fit with him on that disc sled, the way he felt when the boy looked into his eyes. And the way Sadie's teasing response had turned his world upside down, confirming something he'd already subconsciously known.

In the middle of the day's highlight reel, an evening, over a year ago, at Jackson's came to mind. Sometime after his brother had announced that Mackenzie was pregnant—at the time devastating news because he and Mackenzie were not together—Connor had asked Jackson what he was going to do.

"Be a dad?" Jackson had said. "Figure out how to take care of her—of them."

On the heels of that, Connor also recalled what Jackson had said even before that hard moment, in the Storm Café at Christmastime, responding to Connor's challenge of Jackson's pretending that his marriage to Mackenzie was one of love.

"What if it started with commitment?" Jackson had countered.

In the quietness of the night, that statement resounded in Connor's heart. Could he make that kind of commitment? To Sadie, to Reid?

As he thought of that little boy tucked up against his chest, saying good night, he knew with certainty his answer.

His heart already had.

Chapter Nine

(in which choices are made)

Sadie usually fell asleep without trouble. Exhaustion had a strong undertow, one that rarely yielded to any resolution of her mind.

That night, her mind won, and it wasn't a good thing. Rather than replay the way Connor had pinned her with his intense green gaze or relive the stupid thing she'd suggested in jest, she'd rather have gone into that dark oblivion.

You could marry me. Four dumb words stuck on replay, causing her to wilt under her own contempt. Why had she let those words cross her lips? Why had they even been in her head to begin with? The last thing she wanted was to feel more pathetic, more scorn worthy, to the people who had a front-seat witness to her greatest failures in life. And Connor?

Connor knew *everything*. The man should have done an about face the moment he'd seen her drive back into town. If not then, then at least the second those selfish, idiotic words had left her tongue.

But he hadn't. He'd sat there, his gaze narrowed on her face and a terrifying willingness bleeding into his silence.

He wouldn't, would he?

Sadie squeezed her eyes shut as a burn touched her skin. As she couldn't avoid thinking about it, she realized how ridiculous that question was. Yes, honor-bound Connor Murphy would do exactly that. Hadn't he already inconvenienced his life significantly just to see her? To apologize, then to make sure she was okay and to spend time with her son? If he felt even the slightest hint of duty's call toward her, Connor would marry her.

The thought sank into her like hot lead, and her stomach

turned, even as a place deep in her heart melted with something altogether *not* unpleasant. The contradicting reactions whipped up confusion and more restlessness.

What had she done? What would she do?

Gripping the peppermint-scented quilts with tight fists, Sadie breathed a quivering breath and sighed into the chilly darkness.

"Lord, help," she whispered.

***

Connor met the sunrise as it timidly pried the night away from the eastern sky. As he watched the pale-yellow push against the darkness, he wondered if Sadie had slept or if she'd danced with relentless thoughts, as he had.

He hoped she hadn't. But he didn't regret his sleepless night. Once he'd accepted that there would be no rest until things were settled, he'd spent much of it in his dad's worn leather chair, praying. Surrendering himself, asking for wisdom, and for Sadie's peace. Maybe even for her cooperation—because if her response yesterday was an indication, she'd yet to have the same sense of rightness about what Connor planned next.

Didn't mean he wasn't moving forward though.

Resolve grew with the increasing light. After he brewed a fresh pot of coffee, drank a mugful while peace regained control in his heart, then changed into a fresh pair of jeans and a button-down shirt, Connor crept through the sleepy house to leave. It was still early—the younger boys were just finishing showers as they readied for another day of school, and Dad had only moments before sank into that leather chair with his Bible in hand.

"Where you headed, son?" The gravelly sound of his dad's quiet morning voice had held an undercurrent of concern, catching Connor right before he'd tugged open the front door.

With a straight posture, Connor answered in a hushed tone. "There's something I need to take care of."

"Something I should worry about?"

Seemed Mom and Dad were quietly concerned about Connor's new involvement with Sadie. They hadn't said anything outright, but their tight-lipped expressions and silent exchanges of furrowed brows told Connor they were not entirely on board with whatever it was Connor was doing—and not telling them about.

Connor hadn't been one to lie to his parents. The few times he'd been sneaky with his life choices hadn't settled well with him, and they hadn't worked out super great either. But he wasn't sure he could explain this to Dad just yet.

"You sure could pray for me."

"Care to share some specifics?"

Connor looked to the wood floor at his feet. After a slow inhale, he rubbed the back of his neck, then looked back to his dad. "Not yet. But I will, Dad. Promise."

A moment of connection, strong and anchoring, held between them as Dad sustained a look of concern, but also trust, on him, and then nodded. "Okay."

"Thanks."

After that, Connor slipped from the quiet Murphy house.

The crisp morning smelled of things new. New life, new hope. Connor filled his lungs as he stepped down the deck stairs and then toward his vehicle. There would be challenges—the first of which was to convince Sadie—but with each breath, rightness sank deeper, firming his resolve.

He spent the miles that separated his childhood home from hers asking for the right words. Though he felt peace about this decision, the moment he turned into her drive, a strong case of nerves crashed onto him. Muscling through them, Connor fisted and unfisted his trembling hands as he made his way to the Allens' front door, knocked, and then waited.

***

With a hot mug of apple cider cradled in her hands, Sadie leaned against the cushioned back of her chair. At long last she'd drifted into a fitful sleep, one full of random dreams that left only vague impressions of her neediness and Reid's uncertain future. She'd woken with a headache and a vast and desperate emptiness in her heart. Watching the sunrise did not offer the usual calm recentering that she'd come to expect in her adult life.

A tap at the door only caused the anxiety in her heart to

tighten. Even while she wondered who would be visiting so early in the morning—her parents and Reid were still snuggled in their warm beds—her gut clenched with a knowing.

She pulled the door open as if a prowler might be on the other side—slowly and with a sense of dread. There he stood, tall and handsome as ever, causing a zing to ricochet in her chest. He looked anxious, fists clenched and eyes every bit as intense as they had been when he'd left the night before. Sadie wasn't sure she was prepared for what instinct told her he was there for.

"Connor..."

She tugged on her mother's oatmeal sweater, wrapping it tightly around her body as if it could shield her from more than just the morning cold. Connor froze, looking as if he'd just had the wind knocked from his lungs with an invisible blow. Under his unwavering gaze, she became self-consciously aware of how she hadn't yet brushed her hair or fixed her face. She stood before this man she'd once dreamed of as raw as if she'd just climbed out of bed. Which she practically had. At the thought, she drew her brows inward.

Connor stepped closer, reaching to hold her arm with a firm but gentle touch. "I kept thinking about you all night—couldn't sleep."

All her fears had been reality. Sadie shut her eyes and sighed as a battle roused in her heart. "I was worried about that. Connor, I was—"

"I know you were teasing." He edged nearer still, raising a hand to brush his thumb over her cheek. He sounded breathless but determined in a way that sent a flutter of pleasure zipping through her veins. "But I'm not. I think we should."

Her lips parted, but nothing came out. *Should?* It wasn't really a question—she knew exactly what he was talking about. But there was a needy part of her that yearned desperately to hear him say it. Like he *wanted* to say it. And that yearning was painful.

"What?" she finally squeaked.

"I think we should get married." His voice lowered to an intimate quality that tempted her to believe things she knew weren't true.

This is duty. And guilt. Not...romance.

Stepping back, she closed her mouth and shook her head.

"It feels right, Sadie." Connor moved into the space she'd pried between them. "Reid needs a dad, and you need—"

There's the truth. Dashed away was the fanciful dream of hearing *I'm in love with you, Sadie. I want to build a life with you.* A dream she'd known would never be reality—not after what had happened with Ivy, and especially not now, with her advanced cancer diagnosis.

She winced against the slap of reality, but lifted her chin. "I don't want to be your obligation."

"My—" His expression folded into something dark and insulted.

Sadie pushed his touch away. "You have no duty where I'm concerned, Connor. I'm not your responsibility." She wanted to weep—though she wasn't sure it was because she felt so pathetic or because she was tempted to take whatever he offered her and make believe it was everything she used to dream of. Imagine that this bleak future would somehow morph into a beautiful shared life between them.

"Do you think I do things just because I feel obligated to?" He slipped another stride closer, closing her in between himself and the house.

Being cornered like that should have made her feel intimidated. Instead, she felt protected in his shadow. And wanted. Both of which were unreasonable. She ran her bottom lip under her teeth, not trusting herself to respond.

"What I do, I do because I believe it's right." He leaned closer. "You need help. Reid needs a father." Once again his fingers brushed her face, and then he cupped her neck with both hands, conviction a deep current in his voice. "I believe this is right, Sadie."

Her attempt to blink away tears only released them. How could tender emotion and jagged agony run parallel in her heart at the very same moment? "You're banking on me dying, Connor. That this idea won't be permanent for you. How do you expect me to respond to that? With gratitude?" Honestly, there was a big part of her that wanted to. But, oh goodness, this hurt too.

He flinched, as if he felt the tip of that spear as well. "You think I want you to die?" With the gentlest touch, his thumbs traced the lines of her jaw.

Sadie yearned to lean her head against his chest. *What if I said yes?* Could she accept the kind of affection that grew from his dutiful sense of pity? Short term, probably. But...

"What happens if I beat the odds?"

He'd be stuck with her, and how could she live with a man she adored as she did Connor, knowing that he was only with her because of a twisted, overactive sense of obligation?

"Then we'll rejoice. How could you think I *want* you to die?"

"You wouldn't do this if you didn't know that I'm sick."

He shook his head. "There's no way to know that, is there? This is what we have. Sadie, I've prayed for you for years. Do you really believe that that kind of an investment comes with indifference? I care about you. Without hesitation, I can promise that I'll be committed to you as my wife. I've seen what a good husband looks like—I've watched my father be one to my mother. I don't want less, not for you and not from myself. No matter how long we have together."

He kept saying that—*we*. As if it was a done deal. As if she'd said yes.

But he hadn't asked her.

A spark of resentment flashed, adding a new element to her emotional storm. Sadie gripped his wrists and pushed his hands away. Though her eyes still burned with tears, she pointed a glare at him and shook her head. Then she turned and moved to go back inside.

With a sideways step, he shadowed her, his large hand catching hers as she reached for the door.

"Sadie, why are you angry?"

"That's hardly a proposal, Connor Murphy." She wrapped her arms around herself, shielding her body from the cold. And from him. "Just because I'm vulnerable, and you've been nice to my kid, doesn't mean that—"

With gentle insistence, he tugged her back around. Those dark-green eyes were all remorse and so heartbreakingly steady on her, she could hardly think straight. When he silently moved to kneel on the wood decking dusted with snow, Sadie lost it. All the while, he continued to hold her hand.

"Sadie Allen, will you marry me?"

I could say yes... It didn't take much effort for her to make believe in that moment. Actually, it took more effort for her to keep what was real in her mind. Her lips wobbled as she finally summoned the answer she knew was right.

"I think we should think about this, Connor."

"I've done my thinking, Sadie. It may not look like anything either of us thought, but you and I could build a life. I know we can." He slowly stood, still holding her hand. He tucked it against his chest. "But if you need time, then take it. Because I'm not talking about a short-term commitment. I mean husband and wife. As long as we both shall live. And honestly, I hope that's a long, long time."

After a long, searching look, Connor slid a half step back. Then he lifted her hand until her fingertips met his warm lips. And then...

Then he was gone, leaving her in a beautiful devastation.

Chapter Ten

(in which Sadie gives an answer)

Connor stared across the night-dusted town, dotted in a grid pattern with streetlamps and porch lights. Driving back to his apartment near the base had felt like moving toward a vacant wasteland. He hadn't heard from Sadie all day, and it had put him a sour mood, to say the least.

"Are you okay?" Mom had asked more than once.

He'd given her the standard *fine* answer people issued when actually, no, he was not okay. Why was Sadie being stubborn about this? He'd prayed, felt certain of God's direction in his proposal. What reason could there be in making an awkward situation worse?

"Son." Dad had caught him near his Pathfinder when Connor was tossing his overnight bag into the backseat.

Connor had rolled his shoulders back and faced his father as if he were addressing a superior officer. "Sir?"

"I know you said you couldn't share with me yet..."

"No, sir."

"I just wanted you to know that I'll be praying for you. And when you're ready, I'm listening."

"I know that, Dad."

Replaying the way his father had pulled him into a strong hug, unashamed of the bond they shared, Connor gripped the railing to his balcony and shut his eyes.

Dad was his hero. In Connor's memory, Dad had always been their superman. He loved God, loved his wife and kids, was a good provider and an even better example. Connor longed for nothing less than to be like his dad.

Having failed in doing so in high school had left Connor as a young man unmoored, tossed into crashing waves of disappointment and self-derision. It'd taken years of rebuilding to gain a sense that maybe Connor could still rise to the standard his father had lived out. Now, with Sadie and Reid, Connor felt that honorable calling grow stronger.

He wanted to be the kind of husband and father his dad was. With them.

But Sadie...

Connor sighed, folding himself onto a creaky chair as he thought back over the morning. Sadie had been insulted. He rolled his fists together as he pinpointed what she'd resented most about his offer—that he was banking on her death. The memory of her accusation made him feel sick. Did she really think he was that stone hearted? Did she not understand that he—

His thoughts were cut short by the ding of his phone, alerting him to a text.

Do you think you can love Reid?

Breath caught in his lungs as he read her question. His hand quivered as his heart throbbed. *I'm already halfway there.*

He considered adding more but chose instead to wait for her next question, certain it would be about her. Could he love her?

They would never have the Americanized ideal of romance. But he was already loyal to her. He already owned a grounded resolve to take care of her. To be good to her. Long term, wasn't that more stable than romance? Seemed like it should be worth more than momentarily sweeping a woman off her feet, only to leave her flattened by disillusion because the fickle nature of such emotion had been brushed away.

What will happen when I start treatment?

Connor blinked at the screen, not understanding her question. *I don't follow, except to say that I'll take care of you and Reid.*

Where? You'll still have to work. What happens if you're reassigned? It would be better for Reid if we were with my parents.

He hadn't thought that far. Only so much as to imagine it'd be easier for her to recover from treatments—however that looked—in the same town where she received them, rather than traveling back to Sugar Pine. His apartment was fifteen minutes from the treatment center she'd be going to. But he still had a couple months left on his contract. However, there were provisions. He just needed to look into them further.

That would only qualify, though, if Sadie were his wife.

I'm sure that there are provisions for sick leave to care for an ill spouse. I've never needed to look into that much, so I don't know the details. But I'll check.

Seemed like a flimsy response, especially after he'd told her he'd thought this through. Feeling the need to somehow recover what he imagined was a slip in her slim confidence in his plan, Connor quickly typed another text. *My contract is up in three months. I won't be renewing.*

Within only a few beats, she sent a reply. *What will you do then?*

He hadn't any idea. Up until this past weekend, he hadn't even been sure about separation from the air force. But clearly Sadie wanted to be in Sugar Pine in the long run, and that made sense. Having her parents there to help would make things easier, and certainly they'd want to have her close by for as long as possible.

I could see if my dad can take me on. I think he could—especially after Tyler's accident. If he can't, I'll find something else in Sugar Pine.

The minutes ticked by as he waited, anxiety building in the silent space where she didn't respond. Finally, he tapped out her name as if it were an SOS. *Sadie?*

I'm here.

Her words brought a smidge of comfort.

Are you going to marry me? he texted.

The three scrolling dots rolled, feeding the apprehension in his gut.

We can make it work. I swear, Sadie—we'll figure it out.

It's almost like this is what you actually want.

He breathed a hard chuckle at those words. Was this what he wanted? He was sure set on it. Because it was the right thing. Though he had no doubt about that claim, a space of emptiness crept in behind the thought.

Romance was vastly overrated. Besides, Jackson's marriage was working—and that started off way worse than this one would.

If Jackson could somehow grind out what had been a very stupid mistake in Vegas into a marriage of commitment, a real relationship, Connor could claim hope of a promising future.

With Sadie as his wife, Connor's future looked really, really hard. That reality shook some of his surety. How could he forge into a future when he knew there was a possibility it was going to end with deep grief?

One day at a time, he thought, still not typing it out to Sadie but keeping it to himself. *Just do the right thing one day at a time.*

Connor squeezed his eyes shut as he gripped his phone and prayed for the strength and resolve to do exactly that. Then he went back to texting Sadie. *It is.*

Maybe that was by default—he wanted to marry her because he didn't want to live with the regret and guilt he felt certain would find him if he didn't. He didn't want to wake up each day thinking that he hadn't been willing to obey something he felt strongly God was asking him to do. Did that make it a bad thing?

Okay.

Blinking, Connor reread that simple word. What did it mean, exactly? *Okay?*

Yes.

Still not clear. *Yes? You'll marry me?*

Yes.

Into the places that had felt frustrated, and even a little wary, a euphoria seeped. She'd said yes.

They were getting married. Standing, Connor grinned, squeezing his phone with a hand that shook. In normal life, this was the moment he would have swept her up into a joyful, excited embrace. Kissed her. Maybe she would have cried a little. And they would hold on to each other as they thrilled about a life and a future together.

Instead, he was alone on his balcony, only his cold phone in his grasp. A sudden ache of loneliness washed over him.

He prayed their marriage wouldn't feel so empty.

***

She'd said yes.

Alone in the house, tucked beneath a heavy crochet blanket and with a half-empty mug of ginger tea, now lukewarm, waiting on the table beside her, Sadie drew in a long breath. Mom and Dad wouldn't be back for more than an hour. They'd taken Reid to Wednesday night church, and Mom had mentioned something about ice cream afterward. So Sadie had time to gather her bearings.

When would she tell them that she was going to marry Connor Murphy?

Nausea churned in her gut. She was pathetic, taking advantage of Connor like this. What had happened to her levelheaded resolve that had seen her through the day he was physically there, down on one knee, offering the sacrifice of his life to her?

She shouldn't be doing this.

But Reid... The thought came from deep within, almost as if it were not her own, and it calmed the surge of panic that had made her sick.

She had prayed about this over the past few days. It took work to set aside the little girl wound in her heart because the one and only proposal she'd ever receive in her life was issued out of pity and duty and not out of love for *her*. But she'd done that heart labor of laying aside hurt feelings and disappointment and saw Connor's offer for what it was.

A promising future for her son, no matter what happened to her.

There, determination re-rooted. Though she would never have Connor's heart the way a woman longed to, she knew without doubt that her son would be well loved by the father Connor would be. That was worth everything.

Even a marriage of *inconvenience*.

Chapter Eleven

(in which others must see reason)

"You're going to have to say that again."

Sadie squirmed in her chair, thankful that while she had considered telling Reid about what was around the corner in their lives, she had opted to take on what was sure to be the opposition first. Although, she hadn't expected the greatest pushback to come from her mother.

If mortified had a face, it would be Mom's in that particular moment. The moment following Sadie's timid announcement. Dad looked shocked. But not mortified. Mom...

Mom was astounded. And not in a *Oh! I'm so pleasantly surprised and happy for you* sort of way.

"Sadie Louise Allen," Mom pressed when Sadie remained mute. "You look your mother in the eye and say that again."

Sadie cleared her throat, pushing away that sense that she was twelve years old and had been caught doing something terrible. With a quick breath out, she forced herself to do as her mother asked—look her dead in the eye and make her announcement loud and clear.

"I'm going to marry Connor Murphy." Blast, but her voice wobbled on the word *marry*.

Mom's mouth fell open, as if that were the first time she'd heard the news. "Sadie..." she breathed while a scowl forced itself deeper onto her expression.

"Now Eleanor," Dad said softly.

Ah. An ally. With a relieved smoothing of her mouth, Sadie

turned her attention to her dad. That momentary softness of ease left as quickly as it had landed. Dad didn't offer an encouraging smile; rather, his brow was every bit as crumpled as Mom's, and his eyes held deep concern.

"You can't be okay with this, Sadie," Mom said.

Dad shook his head, look lingering on Sadie. "I would not say that, no."

Sadie's stomach twisted, and she wrapped her sweater closer against herself, as if that would ease the discomfort.

Slowly, Dad pulled out a chair from the dining table and lowered himself onto it. He then reached for Mom, gripped her hand, and gently tugged until she also sat at his side.

"We're listening," he said.

Swallowing, Sadie nodded. Her hands folded and then twisted, and she swept through her mind for all the logical whys she'd prepared for this talk. Only one surfaced easily.

"He asked me to."

"This was Connor's idea?" Dad tipped his face thoughtfully.

His comment, though made gently, stung. As if the plan would have more merit if Connor had come up with it. More, the truth also added to the barb. *Sadie* had mentioned marriage first. But she'd been teasing. *Honest, God. It was a mindless slip. I didn't mean for him to take it seriously.*

But Connor had. And he was set on it.

Sadie cleared her throat. "He came here Sunday morning before he left town and...and he proposed." Down on one knee and everything, eventually.

"This is very sudden, Sadie." Mom spoke with a calm directness. "All of this between you and Connor is very sudden."

"Seemed like both of you were in favor of his attention when he first showed up at Christmas."

"He's come every year since you've left. We wanted him—actually both of you—to finally find resolution for the burdens you carry. And to be honest, your dad and I like him quite a lot. If things were different..."

"Things." The word felt like lead falling from her tongue, and

Sadie crumpled onto the chair across from them. "Things like me having cancer?"

Mom winced and then looked nervously at Dad.

"Is that why you're doing this, Sadie?" Dad asked.

She had to pull in another breath, grit her teeth, and blink away emotion before she could answer. "Yes."

That was the bare truth of it, and she might as well just say it.

Compassion softened Dad's face more—Mom's as well—but he shook his head. "I'm not sure that's wise."

Sadie could no longer look at them. She stared at her fingers as they lay upon the table, her heart sinking under the heavy confirmation of what she'd already known to be true. This was not a great idea—it wasn't fair to Connor.

Nodding, she sniffed and then forced her eyes back to them. "I know. Trust me when I tell you I wrestled with this and argued with him. But Reid..." She couldn't finish.

"We're here for your son, Sadie." Mom reached across the table to grip her hand. "For both of you."

Again, she nodded. "I know that. But Connor is willing to be a father to him." There was that resolution again. The anchoring reason that she was determined to do this, even with her parents' disapproval. "He'll be a good dad."

At that, Mom's face lost all hardness and disapproval, and with eyes glazed, Dad nodded. "No one is arguing that."

"I have to make sure Reid is taken care of, especially now that I know how serious the cancer is. Connor has offered to make sure of it—he's practically insistent on it. I've tried to convince him otherwise, but at the end of the day, I have to admit that he's right. The best thing for Reid would be to have a father, a good man who will love him and take care of him and allow you to be Reid's grandparents, no matter what happens to me."

For a long stretch, silence fell between them. Then Dad leaned forward. "What about you though? Marriage is no small thing."

Pain spiked into her heart. How lovely would it have been to say with a dreamy smile that she and Connor were in love, that this intertwining of their lives was because of the romantic, starry ideas that she'd ever read about or seen in epic love stories?

That was not the truth, and the feeling of missing something beautiful was a sharp ache in her chest.

"Reid is worth it." Worth the humiliation of knowing that the man she was to marry did not love her—that there was a very real possibility that his heart had and forever would belong to one Miss Ivy Levens. Her son's future was worth the awkwardness of a marriage that wore more like a business suit than a lovely dress. Reid was worth the sacrifice.

One that Connor was willing to make as well.

"Sadie." Mom spoke timidly now, her gaze nervous and maybe a little guilty. "What if..."

Sadie knew the course of that thought, and she finished it for her mom. "What if I *don't* die?"

How horrible was it that she and Connor were making plans based on the possibility of her shortened life? But she too had asked that very question. Connor's answer had seemed almost a platitude to Sadie, but perhaps that was because she herself did not consider the possibility relevant. The odds were simply not in her favor.

"It must be considered," Mom whispered. "Because it is what I am praying and hoping for." And then the tears came. Mom's. Dad's. And Sadie's.

It was a hard business, this preparing for one's death. For Sadie, it was a required business. But one that, beautifully, graciously, she did not have to do alone.

Because she had her son and her parents. And now, most surprisingly, Connor Murphy.

***

Tired from another day of intense responsibility on base, Connor strode from his kitchen toward the door to his apartment, wondering with an undercurrent of resentment who was unexpectedly on the other side. Even if he wasn't separating from the air force in a matter of months, he would have been seeking a new career path. Working in the tower had worn on him—so much stress every day. Precision and quick decisions, being responsible for the welfare of every jet or plane that took off or landed on his watch.

The burden was heavy, and he was looking forward to laying it down. Particularly at that moment, when he realized he was excessively grumpy at whoever had just knocked on his door when he should be hospitable. Mom had not raised him to be this kind of selfish man.

With a quick inhale to settle his riotous mood and a plea sent heavenward for renewed energy and a Spirit-filled kindness, Connor reached for the doorknob and pulled.

"Dad." He swung the door open fully after he glimpsed his father's face.

Dad wrangled up what Connor was certain was a false smile. "Hello, son. I was hoping you'd be home. Are you in for the night?"

Connor motioned toward the interior of his apartment while he stepped back to allow his dad to pass by. "Yeah. Just got in a few minutes ago."

"Good." Distraction weighted Dad's voice. He walked into the small living space that held a secondhand leather couch and a brown overstuffed chair. The rise and fall of Dad's shoulders was telling, and then Dad planted his hands on his hips and turned around. "Been a while since I've been here."

"Yeah." Connor swallowed. "It's a couple hours' drive, so..."

"Right." Dad's hands slipped from his hips and hung loose at his side. Then he rubbed the line of his jaw.

"Dad?"

"Yeah."

"You made a two-hour drive, and you weren't sure I was going to be here?"

"I was hoping..." He cleared his throat. "The thing is, I think we need to talk."

Connor lifted his brow. "Everything okay? Mom, the boys—"

"About this thing with you and Sadie."

Connor's heart clenched hard in his chest as a wash of heat ran over him. "Sadie..."

"We hear you're getting married." Dad's eyes pinned on him with sparks.

"I...um, well, yeah. We...Sadie and I...I mean, I asked her."

"To marry you?"

"Yes."

"Why?"

Such a pointed question seemed out of place for this kind of conversation. Worse, it felt like a setup—or a scolding.

"How do you know about this?" Connor asked, and then wished he hadn't. He didn't want to make things worse by making it seem like his engagement was some big scandal he was ashamed of. It wasn't. But this wasn't the way he'd wanted his parents to learn about it, either—whatever way that was.

Dad scowled, but the expression seemed more worry than angry. "Eleanor called your mother this morning. She wanted to know how we were handling the news, and what our thoughts about this development were."

Air rushed from Connor's lungs. "Oh." He should have known. He should have made time to talk to Mom and Dad about this before he'd left on Sunday. But he hadn't felt ready to defend his choice to his parents when he hadn't yet convinced Sadie that it was a solid plan.

"She's quite upset."

"Who? Sadie?"

"No, your mom. And actually, Eleanor didn't seem well set with this either."

In the swirl of his discomfort, an edge of defense emerged, feeling more like anger than it probably should. He was trying to do the right thing, a good thing. Why was everyone making him a villain about it? Jamming forked fingers into his short hair, Connor wrestled against the urge to lash out against what felt like an unfair attack.

"Look, Dad. I just got home, and work was pretty stressful. I need a shower and some food before I'm going to be able to have this conversation."

Pressing his lips closed, Dad studied him for a moment and

then nodded. "Fair enough. I'll go get us something to eat, how about?"

Drawing a breath, Connor nodded. "That'd be good, thank you." He moved toward the hallway that led to his bedroom and bath.

"Connor?"

He stopped but didn't turn.

"I'm not here to attack you."

With a glance over his shoulder, he nodded. "That's good to know, Dad."

Twenty minutes later, somewhat calmed by a hot shower and the inviting aroma of Chick-fil-A, Connor lowered onto a chair across the room from where his dad had landed. Dad bowed his head, and Connor followed his lead, listening while his father thanked God for the food, for Connor and for Sadie, and asked for wisdom for them all. It kind of sounded like a lead-in for a redirective lecture. Connor made his own silent appeal for wisdom for this conversation—as well as calm strength to stay the course he believed God had set him on without becoming defensive and ugly about it.

They plowed through crispy chicken sandwiches and waffle fries before another word was spoken, the quiet hovering in the space feeling like the wary moments Connor had experienced before he'd jumped out of a plane back in Germany. That hadn't been required—more like a benefit to being an airman working with flight crews at that particular time and place. The feeling had been all fear and anticipation, knowing the next few moments could be life changing. For good or for bad. That jump, however, had been optional—and honestly *didn't* have the sort of life impact marriage would. This conversation, and the action that was forthcoming, they weren't optional. Connor knew it in his gut and heart.

Marrying Sadie, being Reid's dad, these were his new commissions, and his life would never be the same.

"Talk to me, Connor." Dad brushed his fingers off onto a napkin, loosely threaded his fingers, and then leaned forward onto his knees. "Help me understand this decision."

With a deep draw of air, Connor tried to sort his words so that he'd make sense. He'd make his dad see what he saw. "You know that Sadie has always been on my heart, my mind."

"I know you've felt responsible for what happened between Ivy and Sadie. You've taken flowers and apologies to their families for years—which to be honest, I've had a mixed feeling of pride in your dedication and caring heart and concern for this overbearing sense of responsibility you carry. Son, it's been a long time—and Ivy's death *wasn't* your fault."

"I know that. But she died angry with me. Legitimately so. And Sadie, she's carried a burden that I had a big part in making worse for her. When Ivy died, all chances for those two to reconcile died with her. That's a tough thing to live with, and I was part of it."

Lines carved into Dad's forehead as he listened. "I get it, Connor. But what about forgiveness? God's, specifically. I know you've laid this sin before Him and asked for His forgiveness. But it's like you keep living as if God can't give that to you. You know that's wrong, right?"

Connor shook his head. "You've got it wrong. That's not what this is."

"Then explain it to me, because this choice—this idea of marriage—from your mother's and my view, it looks like it's being driven by all levels of negative emotion, and that's worrying us."

He drew another fortifying breath, praying for steadiness. Reaching for wisdom. "Sadie is special to me, Dad. I've prayed for her for years, for her heart's healing. For God to intervene on her life so that she wouldn't live broken and reckless. Because I know what it's like to feel like you've messed up not only your own life but other people's, and there's no way to fix it." The crispness of his voice wavered on that last sentence.

"That's what I'm talking about, Connor. This sounds like guilt."

He shook his head. "It's not. I promise, Dad, this is not being fueled by guilt. I told you, she's special to me. How could she not be when I've petitioned heaven for her for so long? That's not negative, and it's not guilt-driven responsibility. It's honest and deeply rooted."

"Okay..." Dad nodded slowly, still very much skeptical. "Then maybe you should try dating her for a while. See if this leaning you have toward her grows into—"

"She's sick, Dad. Maybe dying. That's why she came home." Connor held a steady look on him, all unmovable resolution. "I don't feel like we have that time or luxury. Here's the bottom line: I feel, in my spirit, a God-directed call to be Sadie's husband while she walks through this battle with cancer. And I *know* that Reid needs a father. One like I had."

Emotions morphed on Dad's face, going from concerned uncertainty to empathy and then to tenderness. His eyes glazed with a telling sheen when Connor finished. For many moments, quiet settled in the room while Dad processed the full reality. He swallowed hard more than once.

"I see..." he finally whispered.

"Do you?"

Dad sighed. "I do see. I still can't say that I'm sure you're right. But I can't say that you're wrong either. You've prayed about this?"

"I have—almost since the day she came back. Though not specifically about marrying her, but about what God would have me be to her and to Reid."

"Connor, this isn't just a short-term inconvenience..."

"Don't call it that." Connor's response came sharp. "Don't call Sadie that, or Reid."

Dad hung his head, and after a pause, he nodded. "I'm just saying it will be hard."

"I'm aware of that. But I'm not banking on her death, looking forward to when I'll be a free man again. Don't paint me as that kind of guy. The idea of her not making it hurts. It already hurts."

Chapter Twelve

(in which Sadie and Reid visit Connor)

Come home and talk to your mom. She needs to hear your heart.

That had been Dad's parting words, after they'd gone through Connor's reasons and then prayed together over the future and the families. It had come almost as a relief that Connor couldn't go that weekend because he was scheduled as backup for the tower. Also, he'd asked Sadie if she and Reid would come to his place on Saturday so that they could talk details.

He'd need to be armed with those details before heading back up to Sugar Pine, because he had a feeling Mom wasn't going to be as ready to hear his logic as Dad had been. Lovely woman that she was—and make no mistake, Connor adored his mother—she was a hard-core romantic, and clearly she didn't sniff romance in his engagement to Sadie. She smelled obligation. And guilt. And possibly trouble.

Did she know how very *un*romantic Jackson's marriage truly was—not to mention how much trouble his younger brother had been in? Deep didn't even touch the level of messiness Jackson's marriage had been from the get-go. If she'd known at the time, Mom would have been horrified and heartbroken for her son.

Right there was something Connor needed to keep in mind, even as he suited up for defense about this marriage he was determined to see through. Mom's heart was all about her boys. She loved them like a fierce mama bear, and they were blessed by her stout spirit. If she was upset with Connor about this, it would be because she feared for his well-being. If she was determinedly opposed to it, it was because she wanted the best for her boy. Sometimes, she just didn't know what that was.

Connor scraped the cooked eggs off the bottom of the pan, plated them, and sprinkled pepper-jack cheese over the top. Not quite as good as the breakfast he could have found at the Storm Café back home, but it was decent protein without a lot of fuss. He took his plate to the bar-style table he'd purchased for his eat-in kitchen and slipped onto one of the stools. Looking at the small round surface of that table, he made a mental note: *get something else*. This wouldn't work for the three of them—particularly for Reid. Certainly the kid could scamper onto the higher stool, but a fall from it would be much worse than a regular chair.

So it began.

Yeah, there would be changes in his life. Replacing a tiny dining set wasn't a big deal. Sharing space? Living together...

They hadn't even nailed down how that was going to look. Thus Sadie coming—he checked his watch—in less than an hour. His stomach twisted in a weird painful-excited sort of way, which oddly gave him a measure of peace. He was excited to see her again—it'd been a week since he'd gazed up at her from bended knee, one of texting back and forth small niceties: *How was your day? How are you feeling? What's Reid been up to? Do anything fun?*

She'd been reserved in her responses, but what could he expect? This wasn't like Matt and Lauren's relationship had been—the pair tossed together in a blizzard and stirred up with chemistry and perfect timing.

Connor wasn't expecting romance, and he doubted Sadie was either. They were in this for the anchor of stability. If Sadie needed a slow tempo toward warming to the idea of him being part of her everyday life, that was fine. He could pace.

Shoveling eggs into his mouth, he had to chuckle at that last thought. Pace. Right. One of the things he and Sadie needed to discuss that day was setting a date. To be married. How was that for pacing?

He glanced toward the living room, which he'd straightened before he'd showered that morning, and let his focus settle on the

Hot Wheels Criss Cross Crash set. Suddenly the nerves inside his stomach morphed into something less exciting and more like nausea.

Reid... What if he didn't like Hot Wheels? Connor couldn't remember seeing cars at the Allens' house the few times he'd been there. He should have gone with Legos. Those were a sure bet, since he'd spent time building a set with the kid over Christmas break.

God, I'm not sure how to be a dad. Most men grow into it, you know?

The eggs in his gut now burned a little, and Connor slid off the stool, carried his empty plate to the sink, and washed it. Who could he ask for advice on the dad thing? Of his six brothers, only three were married. Matt and Lauren had announced they were expecting, but the baby wasn't due until early summer. Jacob and Kate were building the perfect life, except Connor knew from the private conversations he and Jacob had on occasion that everything was not perfect at all. The no-children thing for them wasn't by choice, even if they left that impression with the rest of the family. Jackson and Kenzie had little Bobbie Joy, but she wasn't even walking or talking yet.

That left Dad. A good option, but Connor didn't want his father to backpedal on his tentative support for this microwave marriage.

So Connor would have to figure it out on his own.

He washed and dried the plate and the glass he'd used for orange juice and then put both away. Just as he rolled his wrist to check his watch, a knock clunked from his front door. Since he was already in midmotion, he checked the time. Sadie was early?

Rolling his shoulders back, Connor worked for a relaxed look before he opened the door.

"Mrs. Hunt." He blinked and swept away the surprise-disappointment that must have shouted from his expression as he greeted the wife of one of his fellow traffic control airmen. "Good morning."

Mandi Hunt smiled sweetly, her gentle brown eyes matching

the grin. She was a small woman, bubbly in personality—which seemed to be of great help to Hansen, her husband. He said she was always the balm he needed after a stressful day of keeping planes on schedule and out of collisions. "Good morning, Sergeant Murphy."

"Connor."

"Okay, Connor." She lifted her hands, bringing attention to a foil-wrapped package she held. "You know, Hansen and I were praying the other day, and you came to mind." She laughed, the sound a bit self-conscious. "I don't even know why—I haven't seen you since last fall. But you did. So." The silver thing came higher and toward him. "It's just banana bread. With chocolate chips—because that always makes everything better, including bananas."

Connor chuckled because he couldn't help it. "Thank you, Mrs. Hunt."

She nodded. "If there's ever anything you need, please let Hansen and me know."

"I'll do that."

"Good. Have a good weekend, Connor." The cheerful woman turned, her flash of a grin pointed up at him before she faced away and then scurried down the stairs.

"Mrs. Hunt?"

"How about just Mandi?"

"Right. Mandi." He brushed the tickle of heat toying with his neck. "There is one thing... I'm getting married."

"Oh wow! That's great! I'd love to meet your fiancée."

"Yeah. That's what I was going to ask. I mean, sometime I'd like you and Hansen both to meet her and her son." He felt breathless as he finished, but her pleasant expression didn't falter one bit.

"That would be perfect! How old is her boy?"

"Four."

"Perfect," she said. "Our Liam will be five next month. It'll be great to have a new friend." She nodded, as if to emphasize the point. "For both of us."

And then she was away, leaving Connor with the impression that God was working hard to make sure Connor stayed the course. They were going to be okay. This marriage—it *was* a good idea.

***

Sadie's core shook as she stepped up the final riser and spotted apartment 7. Connor's. Quietly she drew in a long breath and squeezed the small hand warming hers.

"Which is Mr. Sergeant Connor's?"

Glancing down, she tried to absorb the excited energy in Reid's brown eyes. "Number seven. Can you find it?"

He wrinkled his nose and examined the four doors in the small hallway, each with a large silver number anchored in the middle. Reid knew his numbers—at least to ten. They'd been working all the way up to twenty, but Sadie was certain he was solid to ten.

"That one!" One stubby finger pointed up to the first door on their right.

"Smarty guy." Pride made her mouth shift from a nervous frown to a grin. "You got it. Want to knock?"

"Yeppers!" He scrambled forward, hand slipping from hers. His little fist was still clunking on the door when it opened. "Mr. Sergeant Connor!" That little body went ramrod straight as Reid fixed a salute.

"At ease, Airman. I'm just Connor, remember?" Eyeing Sadie with a smile that was both shy greeting and subtle question, he stooped to closer match Reid's height. As he tentatively pulled her son into a hug—one which Reid was all in about—Sadie understood his silent inquiry. Had she told Reid?

No. She hadn't. Not after things had gone more rough than smooth with her parents. It had made her feel unsteady for the rest of the week.

Connor stood straight again, easing Reid into his apartment with his large hand on the little boy's back while his gaze held steady on her. "Hi."

At his low, almost intimate tone, she felt her heart flutter and the warmth of a blush rush her face. "Hi."

One corner of his mouth hitched in a grin that warmed her to the marrow of her bones. *Whatever else he may be*, she thought, *Connor Murphy is one sexy man.*

And he was going to marry her.

As if reading her thoughts—well, maybe not all of them—he reached for her hand, drew her in close enough that the warmth of his body seeped into hers, and pressed an uncertain kiss to her forehead.

"I'm glad you came," he whispered, sounding shy, which triggered another fluttery thrill through her chest.

Why she wasn't sure, but goodness this contradictory blend of shy strength he had going on was like syrup to a hummingbird, and her heart was like the zippy little bird's wings. Beating crazy.

"Mommy, look!" Reid's excited call pulled her out of fantasy world only a breath before she was going to step in closer, fold against him, and immerse herself into the dream that this thing between them was romance.

Good timing. Except, the hard-stop thud of her heart, which ceased the fun fluttery thing that had happened, didn't feel that good. Sadie looked down, hiding her wince, and stepped into Connor's apartment.

"Whatcha got, bud?" She plastered a smile onto her lips as she moved to the living room, where her son was.

"Cars, Mom! Connor has cars!"

"Actually"—the door clicked closed as Connor spoke—"that's for you, Reid. I was hoping you liked cars."

"For me?" Those wide dark eyes lifted beyond Sadie's face to the man who was certainly standing behind her. "Really?"

"Yeah. I'll help you set up the track, if you want."

"Sweet!" Reid shifted his voice to sound like the turtle on *Finding Nemo*. Something Sadie knew her son would only do with someone he felt comfortable with.

Connor had bribed her kid. Clever man. Or desperate.

"Do I get to take it home with me?" Reid asked.

Connor lowered onto the carpet beside Reid, his wary look finding Sadie. "Well, I was thinking that we could keep it here."

Swallowing hard, Sadie pressed her lips together and subtly shook her head. One brow lifted on Connor's well-defined face, and he frowned.

Reid worked the opening of the box, careful not to tear it, contrary to every other four-year-old on the planet. "Will I get to come back to play with it?"

A cool expression passed through his eyes before Connor turned his attention back to Reid. "All the time."

Were his feelings hurt? Or was he just irritated with her for failing to tell her son their plans? Either way, Connor wasn't happy with her. The trembling in her chest returned, and her stomach rolled.

"Do you mind if I get some water?" she asked, hoping she only imagined her voice wobbling.

Connor place a hand on Reid's head and tousled his hair. "I'll be back, okay?"

"I'll keep fixing this." Reid's look was all serious business.

"Good plan." Connor swept up to his feet in one motion and led the way into his small kitchen. "Just water? I have coffee, and I picked up that tea you like."

"You know what tea I like?"

He shrugged. "Ginger spice. You drink it every time I come to your parents' place. Either that, or cider, which I have too."

Sadie bit her lip, swimming in the awkward paradox of appreciating him and being frustrated with him. He was thoughtful and kind. He was pushy and presumptuous. He looked at her like she mattered to him more than she should given their history and the fact that there were all those years of not knowing each other. Then he looked at her like she'd messed up.

Reid was *her* son. She'd tell him when she was ready.

Next thing she knew, Connor had a steaming mug of warm spice in his hand and was passing it to her. "How was the drive?"

"Fine." Sadie sipped her tea, hoping he didn't know she was covering up the fact that she didn't know how to be with him.

With both hands, he gripped the counter behind him and leaned back. "Reid doesn't get car sick?"

"No. He hasn't yet, anyway."

"Lucky guy. One of my brothers—Tyler—he got sick every time we traveled. Mom carried a coffee can with a lid, and he'd use it every trip."

Sadie wrinkled her nose. "That's not fun."

"No kidding. For anyone." Connor made a disgusted face that made Sadie chuckle.

The tension between them eased, and he stepped forward. Reaching to cup her elbow, he guided her into a slow walk beside him. "How about I show you around?"

"An official tour?"

"Right. It'll last about thirty seconds."

He wasn't kidding. The kitchen was an eat in, the living room, where Reid continued to build the racetrack by following the pictorial instructions, was right off both, separated by a small island with barely enough space for a sink and small bit of counter. Down the short hall was the sole bathroom and two bedrooms.

Her lungs felt tight as she peered into the larger master bedroom. His king bed was covered with a plain dark-blue comforter, made neat as a pin with square corners at the bottom. There was an old leather chair in the corner, a single dresser against the wall, and a locker at the foot of the bed. Nothing else. Everything was crispy clean and orderly.

With his arms crossed, Connor leaned against the wall. His silent study weighed on her, and when she turned her attention to him, she glimpsed apprehension in his eyes.

"It's...very tidy."

He flinched but turned his face toward the door on his right, as if to hide his reaction. "This is my office right now, but I'll move everything out. Shouldn't take more than one load to get it all up to Sugar Pine, and I'll store it at my parents'."

Reid's room, then. Sadie swallowed hard. Now they were talking details. She bit her lip as she struggled for a normal breath.

"You haven't told him," Connor whispered.

She shook her head.

"Are you having second thoughts?"

A million of them. But none that could summit the reality that Connor's offer was the best thing she had going for her since Reid was born. And that little boy needed this man. Again she shook her head.

Connor's hand warmed her shoulder, then drifted down until he wrapped his fingers around hers.

"Are you?" She forced herself to find his eyes again.

"No." He pushed off the wall and narrowed the gap between them.

His long gaze made her breathless, and she wondered what he would do if she eliminated the space between them entirely. Such thoughts reminded her that they had things they needed to clear up—expectations he might have that she wasn't sure she could meet.

"Connor, this marriage..."

He waited, his thumb brushing over her knuckles.

"Will we share a room?" she finally blurted, then shut her eyes as flames scorched her cheeks.

For torturously long moments, he said nothing. Then, finally, he moved to grip her other hand. "Reid needs to see me as his dad."

So that was a yes, then? Sadie scrambled for clear logic.

"I really think it'd be easier for you if you lived here for treatments anyway, Sadie. The center is only fifteen minutes away, and you won't have to brave the mountain pass."

"But I moved back to Sugar Pine so my parents could help me with Reid." That had been the only reason she'd found that could force her back.

"I'll be here."

"But you'll still have to work." They'd been over this already. Still at an impasse. Maybe this wasn't going to work at all. When the thought should have given her relief, and an out, she found that it weighted her heart with despair.

"Sadie." His tone commanded her to look at him.

She sighed but did so.

"I'll be your husband, and I'll take care of you."

Suddenly she had to blink. "It's not going to be pretty, Connor."

He nodded, the space between his brows folding. "For better or worse."

"It will be worse. You need to know that reality up front. Already, I have...problems. Embarrassing ones. Things you don't think about, you don't want other people to see."

"I get it, Sadie."

"Do you?"

"I looked up cervical cancer. The symptoms, the progression, the treatment..."

"That's not the same thing as living it."

"I'm sure you're right." He sighed, dropped one of her hands, and stepped back. "But I haven't changed my mind. Maybe you're scared that I expect things you can't give me now." He cupped her jaw and tipped her face so that she'd look at him again. "I don't. Even if you weren't sick, I wouldn't demand something from you that you weren't ready for."

What this man real?

"What's in this for you, Connor?" *Atonement*. The answer slipped into her mind with a subtle toxicity. She shouldn't resent it—after all, he was giving her hope for her son. But she did.

"You. And Reid." His low tone sounded tender, almost loving.

And she was almost convinced that she was wrong about his real motivation. Almost.

She turned her face toward the living room, and his touch slipped away. An emptiness yawned through her at the sense of almost having something beautiful. A near miss that felt almost worse than a total failure. She would have Connor's devotion; of that she didn't doubt. But her greedy heart wanted more.

Reid will have it though. She was pretty sure of that. Very sure of it. And that was worth it. She drew in a breath of courage and looked back at Connor.

"We could tell him together, if you want?" she said.

The lines of worry and confusion melted from his handsome face, and his lips smoothed into a small smile. "I'd like that."

***

Sadie's hand slipped into his, and they walked toward the living room together. Desperately, Connor tried to reassemble his thoughts and put them neatly back into place.

Connor liked predictability. He liked having a plan, feeling like his life was in order. Since Sadie and Reid's arrival, however, he was a vessel in distress. What he'd wanted was to sit down with their smartphones, look at their calendars, and nail down a date to say I do. He'd expected that Sadie was prepared for that next step—meaning that she'd told her son, soon to be his as well—that she was getting married and Reid was getting a father.

The moment he'd discovered she hadn't told Reid yet, Connor felt order slip from his grip. Hadn't it been reasonable to expect that she would have explained things?

Then instead of setting a date, doing the next step, she'd skipped over making things official and worried about other details. Not that those *details* weren't important; they were. Quite. Their sharing a bedroom, specifically, was important to him—but not because of what she'd assumed. Did she really think he'd expect intimacy from her as things stood?

Not the point, anyway. Good grief. Sadie had really knocked his focus off kilter. He needed—*needed*—Reid to see him as his dad. Their entire future depended on that. If Sadie and Reid stayed in Sugar Pine, Connor couldn't figure how that was going to happen. And if Connor spent his nights on the couch, once again, what kind of a picture was that going to paint for a four-year-old kid?

Slow down and think. One problem at a time.

Chaos wasn't new to him. His job, though it functioned on schedules and protocols, demanded that he think quickly on his feet. Because those schedules got miffed, and if he didn't figure out how to untangle the messes, lives could be lost.

He could untangle this mess too.

So the next problem: bring Reid in on the mission.

Hand in hand with Sadie, Connor reached the couch in his living room and lowered onto a cushion. Sadie hesitated but then sat next to him.

"Hey, Reid, buddy," she said. "Can you pause your Hot Wheel project for minute. I—we—need to talk to you."

Reid shook his head no. "I'm on a roll, Mom."

"Reid." Connor used a soft but firm tone, gaining Reid's attention, as well as Sadie's. She scowled at him, slipping her hand from his grasp.

Instead of arguing again, though, Reid smiled up at Connor, letting the section of track he was fitting together slide from his fingers.

"Hi there." He grinned, his head tipped to one side and eyes wide with angelic impressionism.

Huh. Despite his serious personality, Reid was quite a little charmer. Connor brushed his hand over his mouth, hiding a grin. Then he cleared his throat. "I need to ask you something, buddy." He waved and motioned to the space between himself and Sadie. "Come over here."

"Am I in trouble?"

"No, sweetie." Sadie shot Connor another scowl, then patted the cushion between her and Connor. When Reid hopped onto the assigned seat, Sadie began again. "You know how your friend Max has a mommy and a daddy?"

"Yep. His daddy sells tires at the aut-o-mo-bile store."

Again, Connor had to suppress a laugh.

"Right. And they all live together as one little family."

Reid twisted his mouth and lifted his brows at his mom, clearly not impressed with this conversation at all.

But it was a good lead-in. Connor turned on the cushion and laid a hand on Reid's shoulder. "What would you think if I became your daddy?"

Those big brown eyes grew wide and round, aimed straight up at Connor. "You could do that?" he whispered.

Sweet pain warmed Connor's heart, and he smiled. "I think we could make that happen. We could be a little family—you, your mom, and me."

Starstruck had a face and it was Reid Allen's. He turned to his mom, all wonder and joy, and whispered, "It's like he's a superhero."

The look Sadie cast from the edge of her gaze was part amusement, part irritation. "Connor is something," she said wryly.

"Let's not get crazy with the pedestal here." Connor lifted Reid and plopped him on his lap, simultaneously scooting to close the gap between him and Sadie. "I asked your mom to marry me, and she said yes. That's pretty brave of her, I think, since I've never done anything like this before."

"You're gonna marry Mommy?"

"That's the plan. Are you good with that?"

"And me? Are you gonna marry me too?"

Connor couldn't stop the chuckle. "Um, well. I guess it's sort of like that. Your mommy will be my wife, and you'll be my son."

Two small hands pressed onto either side of Connor's face, and Reid pulled until they were nose to nose. "And you'll be my dad." His voice was all urgency and insistence.

"You've got it."

Those little hands pressed harder into Connor's face. "Always?"

"Forever, buddy." Connor hauled the little guy in close, and Reid wrapped skinny arms around Connor's neck.

A glance at Sadie gave Connor a moment's pause. Tears glistened her blue eyes, and her brow furrowed. But she lifted a small smile at him. There was conflict in her—he could read it. He wanted with everything in him to chase every scrap of it away. He wanted her to have a happily ever after—and in that moment he swore that he'd do anything he could to see that she got it. Reaching for her hand, he wove their fingers together and lifted her knuckles to his lips. Oh how he wished—hoped—she felt in her heart the same big, beautiful thing that was moving through his.

"We'll be a family," he said again, his gaze steady on her.

She squeezed his hand, nodding ever so slightly. "Okay." Her look slipped to Reid, and when she leaned in, it was the back of her son's head she kissed.

Chapter Thirteen

(in which Connor and Jackson have a talk)

"Is everything settled?" Mom eyed Sadie with lingering hesitation. She'd stopped pressing her point about this marriage being something birthed by all sorts of negative emotion. But she still wasn't thrilled about the arrangement either.

Sadie tugged the edges of that large oatmeal-colored sweater over her teal long-sleeve T-shirt and lowered onto the other side of the couch, where Mom sat. "We set a date. March twelfth."

Mom nodded. "And Reid?"

"Was thrilled. He called Connor a superhero." Sadie ducked her head, her look falling to her fingers gripping the bulky knit of the sweater.

Mom waited a breath and then covered Sadie's knee with her hand. "You don't sound thrilled about that, sweetie."

With a shrug, Sadie tried to push away the unexpected sadness her son's over-enthusiasm had wrought in her. "It's just always been me and Reid, I guess. I'll have to learn to share."

"That will be hard, I'm sure. Especially with the way Reid idolizes Connor right now. But that won't always be the case. First time Connor has to discipline him will likely change things—not that that will be any easier."

Sadie hadn't thought about the everyday practicalities part of Connor stepping into the dad role for her son. Another twist of anxiety shot through her heart. "I'm not sure how I'll handle that."

"So many changes..." Mom eyed her cautiously. "Nothing about any of this is going to be easy."

Raising her gaze, Sadie looked at her mom. "Do you still think this is foolish?"

Mom blinked, then shook her head. "No. No I don't think

that. The more I've prayed about it for the two of you—all three of you—the more I sense that it is God's will. But I still think it's going to be hard. Harder than any of us imagine. And, selfishly, I'm afraid. You just came home, and having you and Reid here has been a joy. I wasn't prepared to let you go so soon."

A sense of being overwhelmed crashed over Sadie. She had to breathe deeply to keep herself in check. Heaven knew she'd cried so much lately, at some point *soon* she needed to be able to grip her emotions and make them behave. Her exhale came out wobbly. "I'm not so sure about moving to his apartment, to be honest, Mom. Connor feels like it's important for us to be a family right away—for Reid to see him as his dad. And he's certain he can take care of us while he's still working on base. But I'm just not so sure..."

"Oh, honey. We'll help you both, I promise. Your Dad and I may not be spring chicks anymore, but we can still travel. Still be perfectly comfortable in a hotel room for a few days."

"So you think Connor is right?"

"Yes, I do think he has a point. And his contract with the air force is only a few more months." Mom laid an arm on the back of the couch and toyed with Sadie's hair.

Sadie felt a twinge of self-consciousness as she thought about the upcoming likelihood that she'd lose her long honey-brown locks. She'd never thought herself beautiful, but unlike most girls she knew, Sadie had liked her hair. She'd liked it long with the way it would naturally roll into big curls at the end. Her mom's mindless touch made her think of the dignity she would continue to lose—and with Connor as her intimate audience to it all.

Her chest squeezed. *Reid. For Reid...*

Almost as if tracking Sadie's thoughts—at least the ones about her son—Mom continued. "Have either of you looked into the state laws regarding adoption?"

Connor had. Along with the full list of things he had laid out for them to discuss, as if this arrangement was something formal and...

Well, it was formal. And rather business-ish. But sheesh.

Connor and his lists. His tidiness and attention to detail. How was the man going to survive living with a four-year-old? Scratch that. How was he going to manage living with her? She was the kind of girl who forgot appointments all the time. The kind who, when presented with a list, instinctively responded with an internal *you're not the boss of me* directed at the offending ink and paper or digital copy. While of a more serious nature than Ivy Levens had ever been, Sadie wasn't the type A kind of girl. Her dad, in fact, had often lovingly called her his *willy-nilly smarty-pants* because she was intelligent and talented but a far cry from organized.

Connor was *clearly* type A. If there was a letter type that came before A, he'd be that.

Her fingers moved from Sadie's hair to her shoulders, and then Mom tugged. Sadie folded into her gentle embrace.

"You'll figure it out," Mom assured. "With prayer and kindness. And love. You'll both figure this out. And maybe it will help to know that while we're still scared about this unexpected new future, your father and I are behind you."

That did matter. Quite a lot. And prayer and kindness she could do. She and Connor both could.

But love? No one said anything about love.

***

Connor curved his arm more securely around Bobbie Joy and sat deeper into the cushions. His niece's coppery eyes looked up at him, total adoration. The little ginger heart-stopper. Then her lids fluttered as she popped her thumb into her mouth.

"She's taken with you, Uncle Connor." Kenzie's voice smiled as she put on her shoes near the door. Connor looked up, catching her grin as she shifted her attention from him to Jackson. "I'll just be about an hour or so."

"No rush, Princess. Bring me back an Orange Julius though." Jackson winked.

Judging by the blush that smeared over Kenzie's freckles, there was a coded message in there somewhere. Connor marveled over the pair of them as he watched. Not that long ago, this had all been a big lie. A massive mistake. Now?

Jackson and Kenzie were every bit as in love with each other as Matt and Lauren were.

Connor bent his head, putting his gaze back onto his nearly seven-month-old niece, and shifted his jaw. A storm brewed inside as he considered his brothers' marriages. Man, he wanted what they had. He definitely did *not* want whatever Jacob landed in though. As of their last conversation, Jacob and Kate's marriage seemed to be on its death bed, and it hadn't been healthy from the start. Connor wasn't sure about all the whys involved in that—Jacob wasn't the confide-everything type, even with Connor. He was the save-face type. The accumulate-and-impress and never-let-down-your-guard type. He also might soon be the divorced type.

It didn't matter that Connor wasn't as close to Jacob as he was with Jackson and Matt. That pending reality made him hurt for his brother. And it made him fearful for his own future.

But there was Jackson.

After hearing the front door quietly click shut behind Kenzie, Connor looked back up to Jackson. The man's eyes lingered on the closed door across the room, a small but telling grin on his face. Yeah, Jackson was flat out in love with his wife.

"You did it," Connor said.

A bit startled, Jackson shifted his attention to Connor. "Did what?"

"Made your marriage work."

A quiet chuckle moved Jackson's shoulders, and he dusted a hand over his head. "I didn't make anything work. God is merciful and good. That's what happened."

"I'll take that. But still. You told me once—well, challenged me actually—that marriage could start with commitment instead of love."

"I remember."

"Seems that you were right."

Jackson rubbed his jaw and thought for a moment. "I can't claim this one, Connor. Like I said, God is good. That's the reality here. Didn't matter for a time how hard I tried. Kenzie was scared of marriage, and she didn't want to be in one. She left me, remember?"

Connor nodded and glanced down at the sleeping baby in his arms. She sighed, her tiny lips moving against her thumb just before it slipped out of her mouth as she surrendered to sleep. It was a miracle—Jackson and Mackenzie and this sweet baby girl. Everything about their story was covered with God's redemptive fingerprints. Now they had this beautiful life together.

There was still the reality that Jackson had started with commitment.

"Connor, Dad says you're getting married."

Connor's brows lifted before his eyes did. "He told you that, did he?"

"Was it a secret?"

"No, not really, I guess."

"Is that why you're here?"

Connor's visits had been less frequent since Bobbie Joy had been born, not that Connor hadn't wanted to come. But he'd seen the shift in Jackson's marriage and wanted to give the newlyweds/new parents space to grow in this emerging beauty they'd found. He lifted a wry grin to his brother. "Am I intruding?"

Jackson rolled his eyes. "Not at all. Kenzie's afraid she's scared you off."

"A little freckle-face pixy like her? You've told her I've survived the military, right? I'm not scared."

Chuckling, Jackson stood, walked the short distance to his kitchen to fill a pair of water glasses, and then returned to hand one to Connor. "You should meet her mom. She's a little terrifying."

Connor snorted, startling Bobbie Joy. With gentle fingers, he smoothed the fine red-brown fuzz of hair over her head, marveling at how massive his hand seemed against her miniature face. "Were you scared the first time you held this one?" he asked, not looking at his brother.

"Petrified. And thrilled. Actually, I cried, but don't tell Matt. It was a pretty amazing day."

"Think Matt will cry?" Early summer was well on its way, and Matt would enter into fatherhood too. To say Mom was ecstatic when Matt and Lauren shared the news at Christmas about her second grandchild would be the understatement of all of Murphy history.

Reid would make three for her. Would Mom love the boy Connor was going to claim as his son as much as she did this tiny scrap of human in his arms right now, or the newborn to come in June?

"Don't know about Matt," Jackson said. "I'm wondering about you though."

Connor looked up. "Me?"

"I hear you'll be an instant dad."

"Yeah. Sadie has a four-year-old son. Reid. He's pretty great."

"You ready for that?"

"I think so. Maybe. I mean, can you really be ready, in reality? Were you ready for this?" He moved his arm to indicate Bobbie Joy.

"No." Jackson's face was only rapture and pure love as he looked at his daughter. Then he sat back and focused on Connor again. "I'm wondering though, why all of the sudden you're engaged to a woman no one has seen in years. And why Mom is not flipping-out happy about it."

"Yeah, good question about Mom. She's not being her usual self about Sadie at all." Connor turned to stare out a window, feeling a frown pull on his mouth. Mom was usually a big lover of all people. There were only a handful of times, of individuals, whom Mom didn't embrace with optimism and ready love. Kate, Jacob's wife, had been one of those isolated examples, and even with her, Mom hadn't started out with a wary attitude when they'd first met. Back when *Jackson* had brought Kate home to meet their mother.

Wow, people and relationships could be really complicated. A fact that confused Connor, and something he usually avoided. He liked neat and tidy things. Systems he could figure out. Situations he could manage.

Mom was not being systematic or manageable about this.

Connor's thoughts circled back to Sadie and Mom's reaction to her. All these years, Mom had supported Connor's diligent maintenance of a relationship with Mr. and Mrs. Allen. With the Levens too, for that matter. She'd always prepared a floral arrangement for him to give both sets of parents and for him to lay at Ivy's graveside, and only allowed him to pay her costs for the product. Every now and again, Mom had asked if he ever heard from Sadie. Every time, when he'd answer that he hadn't but he was still praying for her, she would nod, tenderness in her eyes, and then give him a hug. All indications that she bore no ill will toward Sadie.

But now Sadie was back in Sugar Pine. Back in Connor's life. And Mom was chilly toward her. Or maybe she was simply uncomfortable with Connor marrying her.

"Mom just wants the best for you. For all of us." Jackson relaxed against the chair. "She doesn't want to see you get hurt."

"Life is full of hurt. Can't really avoid that."

"Sure. But this is *marriage*, Connor. That's not like a finger prick—quick and done and you move on with life."

"Look at you, all grown up and wise."

Jackson rolled his eyes.

"Seriously, Jackson, I've thought this through. I've prayed about it."

"Okay, I don't doubt that. But why the rush? I mean, you haven't even dated her—barely even really know her. She's been gone for years, so you can't blame the people who care about you for scratching their heads and frowning at you about this. Why not give it a little more time?"

Bobbie Joy wiggled and stretched, and Connor shifted the tiny warm bundle, snuggling her against one shoulder and patting her back. "Sadie is sick."

Jackson's gaze felt penetrating and alarmed. Probably like Connor's stare had felt back when Jackson told him that Kenzie was pregnant. Man, that had been a curve ball, to say the least. Jackson had been wrung out hard that night, sure that he'd ruined Mackenzie's life and drowning in the shame of it.

"Sick?" Jackson low tone hinted that he understood.

"She has cancer. An aggressive type, and things don't look good."

"Aggressive—as in likely terminal?"

A sudden swell of emotion bowled over Connor, and he could only shrug. He tucked his face toward Bobbie Joy and inhaled her warm baby scent.

Would he ever hold his own infant child like this?

Not Sadie's and mine. The thought wrenched his heart. But instantly it was soothed with the memory of Reid's hand in his. Reid was enough. He would be more than enough, and Connor would love him fiercely.

He already did.

Jackson shifted, the sound rustling the chair. "So this is about the boy, then?"

Though he knew Jackson didn't mean for it to, the question sounded like a trap. Like a way to make Connor see that this was a mistake. He seamed his lips and pointed a chilled look at his brother.

Jackson met the challenge with a raised brow, and then a knowing glint made his brother smirk. "You care about her?"

"I do. Both of them—and don't ever insinuate otherwise again."

The hint of mischief faded from Jackson's expression as he looked toward the floor and nodded.

"Look, Jackson," Connor said. "I'll do what I believe is right, whether I've got you with me on it or not. But it'd be nice if you had my six on this. I was there for you, you know? I'm not being rebellious. Not being impulsive. I'm honestly trying to do what is right and honorable. Sadie needs help—how could I stand back and watch her go through this when I feel a call to do it with her? And if this grim prognosis is accurate, all Reid will have left are his grandparents. What if something happens to one or both of them? Reid has no one else—he'll be an orphan. I can't let that happen, Jackson. My *soul* demands that I *not* let that happen."

When Jackson looked up, it was with admiration. "You were always the one to step forward first. To honor. To defend. To protect. When we were little, I knew you were the brother to run to when the others were mean about my face."

"We're not talking about a scar on your lip. We're talking about a whole life."

"I know that." Jackson held his gaze steady. "Just making sure you do."

"I'm not ignorant."

"Maybe just a little too honor bound for your own good."

"What does that mean?"

Jackson sighed. "First, let's clear this up. I'm with you, Connor. But here's the thing—I can see you already care about Sadie, maybe more than you're willing to admit. You've no idea how hard it is to live with a woman you care about so much and not have her return those feelings."

Jackson had always been more emotionally directed than Connor, so his angle didn't surprise Connor much. "But what about starting with commitment?"

"Commitment doesn't come without emotions, even if you're Connor Murphy. It just can't. That's what I'm trying to tell you here, that at some point you're going to find that your heart is fully involved, and there's a pretty good chance that no matter how Sadie's illness works out, that heart involvement is going to be painful. If it is, it will be really tempting to respond to the gut punch with resentment or with retreat. It will take total humility and full surrender, in fact, to *not* respond that way."

Bobbie Joy squirmed and let out a high-pitched yowl. Connor tipped her forward into his hands, looking at her as she scrunched up her perfect little face into the most heartbreaking pathetic cry. Talk about a gut punch. How could one little miniature person shred his heart with a single breath?

"I'll take her." Jackson had his daughter swept into his arms before Connor could respond, and then he was carrying her down the hall.

That left Connor alone to mull over Jackson's words. Did his younger brother think he was the only Murphy who could do sacrifice? Fact was, Jackson's marriage and resulting struggles were products of self-pity, too much alcohol, and moments of stupidity.

No. Connor tamped down the temptation to have an internal crossed-arm huff at his brother. Jackson spoke from hard experience, no matter what had pushed him there. Over the previous year, Connor had seen Jackson break in ways that few men ever witness another doing, and it had been hard to watch. Jackson warned out of love. And maybe out of wanting to see Connor do this thing well.

He would. Connor would take care of Sadie and Reid. Didn't matter if or how much pain was involved. He would do it like Jackson said—with humility and surrender.

He was resolved to it.

Chapter Fourteen

(in which plans are finalized)

"Is Mr. Sergeant Connor coming today?"

Sadie wasn't sure if she wanted to roll her eyes or laugh. She did both. "I told you at least three times since you woke up at six this morning. Connor will be here."

"When. Now? Is he coming now?" Reid lifted up on tiptoe to peek out the window, looking for his hero to materialize in that very instant.

Sadie knelt beside him and fingered his wispy hair. "I'll tell you when he texts me."

Those big brown eyes, though always serious, gleamed with excitement. "Is he still going to marry us?"

"Yes." Her tummy did a strange delightful flip. Goodness she was off the charts with her emotional swings about marrying Connor Murphy. One second, she was doubting her sanity. The next, resenting that he had already eclipsed her, it seemed, in her own son's eyes. And the next... Well, her tummy did ticklish things that made her heart flutter and her pulse race.

That was just attraction, and it shouldn't surprise her. She'd always thought Connor was one of the best-looking guys on the planet. It had been one of the things that had gotten her into trouble all those years back.

He's marrying me!

The gleeful thought yipped before she could tame it with logic and warning. Connor was marrying her out of pity and duty. She was marrying him out of a fierce love for her son. Attraction didn't figure into that equation, so she'd better get a grip on her yippy, gleeful, romance-craving heart.

"Do I get to call him Daddy?" Reid's soft, almost shy question brought Sadie back out of her head.

Her heart melted. "Yes, buddy. You'll call him Daddy."

Little blond brows lifted with a hint of teasing. "Will he call you honey?"

"No." Sadie's face flamed.

"Sweetie? Pops calls Nana sweetie."

She cleared her throat. "I doubt Connor will call me anything but Sadie, bud."

"Why?"

Rubbing her forehead, Sadie once again doubted the soundness of this plan. It was too late to back out now though. Reid would be crushed. "That's just not how Connor and I are, Reid."

"Sometimes he holds your hand."

"Yes. That's true." How could she sidetrack this?

"And he hugs you."

"Also true."

"And—"

Her phone rang. *Thank You, Lord.* But what had Reid been going to say? Sadie wasn't certain she wanted to know, so she scooted up and across the room to snatch her phone. "Hello?"

"Hey." It simply wasn't okay that the deep tone of Connor's voice, all warm and soft and directed to her, created a current of electrified...something that traveled through her limbs.

He's doing this out of pity. "Hi. Reid was just asking about you."

"I'm about ten minutes from town. I thought I'd stop by my parents quick, if that's okay with you?"

Why was he checking in with her about his plans? "Sure. I didn't expect you'd come straight here."

Silence hung heavy, even over the digital space between them. Had she said something wrong?

"I've been looking forward to seeing you."

Why did he say things like that? This thrill he provoked wasn't fair. "Reid's excited you're coming." She turned her back to her son and lowered her voice. "He wants to know if he can call you Dad."

"I would love that."

"Before we're married?" The bizarreness of this conversation was not lost on her. She wondered if he felt as weird about it as she did.

He hesitated for a minute, leaving her once again wondering if she'd said something he wasn't happy with.

"That's up to you, Sadie. You're his mom."

Squeezing her eyes shut, she shuffled through the practicalities of it, trying to highlight what she thought Connor thought but wasn't saying. He wasn't Reid's dad—not yet. He still had time to back out of this plan that would only cost him. That would shatter Reid's heart, but the damage would be worse if Reid was already calling Connor Dad.

"We'll wait, then. Until...until..." Until Connor couldn't change his mind.

He wouldn't though. Connor wasn't the backing-out sort of man.

Was he?

***

"Mom, we've traveled this road before. I'm not backtracking." Connor crossed his arms, his posture rigid.

"Don't you take a superior stance with me, Connor Murphy." Mom whisked the batter in her mixing bowl with irritated energy. "You can tower over me all you want with your military-earned physique. Your height and breadth will never erase the fact that I am your mother. I've changed your diapers, cleaned up your puke, and wiped snot off your face." She set down her bowl with a *thunk* against the counter and pointed a glare up at him. "Put on some humility, young man."

Connor had a series of flashbacks from his growing-up years. Mom was usually fun, bright, energetic, and good natured. But there was a reason God gave her seven boys. She could handle them. Mightily.

Feeling caught between nowhere good and somewhere

difficult, Connor's posture sagged, and he sighed. He didn't want to be stubborn and disrespectful. Heaven knew he loved his mom. But couldn't she see...

The fire of offense quickly softened in her bright-blue eyes, and Mom drew a calming breath. "Sorry." She stepped forward, closing the gap that was more than just floor space between them, and laid a hand on his arm. "I am calm now. I am listening. Please, for my heart, which is *for* you, my son, tell it all to me again."

"Sadie and I set a date—March twelfth. Yes, I know that is less than two weeks away. Yes, I understand marriage is a lifelong commitment. Yes, I know becoming a father to a four-year-old will be a massive adjustment. Most importantly, yes, I have prayed about this. Often." Connor ended there, holding his study fast on the woman who had indeed wiped snot from his face when he was little, silently begging her to support him. To care for the woman he was to marry. And to thrill at the grandson she would gain. As he watched her struggle with accepting this course of action, he turned and gripped her shoulder.

"Mom. You taught us love. Sacrifice. You showed us with your very life what it looks like." Tears pricked heat into his eyes. "Please...Sadie and Reid both need that."

She visibly swallowed. "I'm not begrudging them that. But I'm worried that you've decided that since your brothers have married and you have not, that this is all you will ever get."

"That I've settled?"

Her wince let him know that she was aware of how harsh that sounded. "I just want you to know the joy of love."

Nodding, Connor wrapped his arm around her and pulled her into a hug. "I know, Mom. Maybe that will just look different for me." He stepped back, catching her eyes again. "I *like* Sadie, you know. And Reid, he's a great little kid." Cupping her elbow, he squeezed. "He could use another grandma, you know. One who loves the dirt, and making stuff, and being wildly creative. One kind of like Bobbie Joy has."

Playfully, she pushed at his chest. "He has a wonderful

grandmother already. Don't go pitting me against Eleanor. She was *my* friend long before you and Sadie..." Another sigh whooshed from her, and she blinked. Then she set her jaw and gripped Connor's hand. "You're really sure?"

"I am."

"You promise you've prayed?"

"Promise, Mom."

Nodding, her gaze drifted from him, the etching of something bittersweet carving in her expression. Then she lifted what appeared to be a forced but resigned smile. "Do I get to be there?"

"At the courthouse?"

"Yes."

Connor hauled her into a fierce hug. "That would mean so much to me."

Her arms wound around him, and it suddenly dawned on him that she seemed small, and that seemed so strange. This person, woman, who had raised him and his brothers—had seen them through untold amounts of injuries, fights, illnesses, mistakes; had fed them like she was feeding an army; had cheered for them; had disciplined them—she was...human. A rather slight woman, actually. One with an enormous heart. And one who perhaps wasn't always perfect.

***

The early afternoon sun made the patches of snow shimmer against the brown and green of earth and trees. Reid darted in and out of the fringes of the woods, finding nature's treasures and running to show them to her and Connor. Mostly to Connor.

Sadie's heart was near to bursting as she watched them interact. She'd overheard Reid's sneaky whisper when Connor had crouched to hug her son earlier that day. "I can call you Daddy. Mommy said so—but not yet. After you marry us."

Good heavens, she'd wanted to let the tears roll. Mostly good tears, especially as she'd watched Connor's reaction. He'd shut his eyes and smiled, holding Reid tight against his chest, and whispered back, "I can't wait, buddy."

Only some of that teary emotion was envy. Just a mite little touch. As was true now, watching Reid run in and out of the trees and then back to the road where Connor walked at her side, delivering sticks and rocks and compacted snow and whatever else his four-year-old hands could find. Of the rush of emotion, only a smidge was jealousy about how much Reid adored Connor—and how much Connor seemed to reciprocate that adoration. Mostly her heart was flooded with awe. And yes, happiness.

They could be happy.

The thought left her startled in the best way. Could she be happy married to a man who had taken her out of a sense of duty and long-held pity? She tipped her chin to glance up at him, and by chance, he looked down at her.

Oh goodness, those eyes. So serious but kind. Warm, and holding her with a steadiness that made her forget to breathe. The lines of his expression eased, and the plane of his firm mouth softened into a tender grin. Suddenly her hand was in the warmth of his, their fingers woven together. Somewhere in this timeless moment, they had stopped walking, and he turned to face her.

"We'll be good together," he said, moving nearer.

When he lifted his hand to run a thumb along the curve of her face, she turned into that soft touch, and a flame flickered in her heart.

"Connor, look!" Reid's yell, the same one they'd heard at least two dozen times during this afternoon walk, came only moments before the little guy crashed into both of them. Short arms wrapped around their legs—one of hers and one of his.

Sadie chuckled, wishing away the heat in her face as she realized that she'd *swooned*—at least nearly so—at Connor's attention. Looking down at Reid, the laugh that she'd used mostly for cover because she was embarrassed became sincere and tender. Connor's hand had fallen from her face to Reid's shoulder, and hers landed on her son's head. Reid held them both, grinning like everything in his world was absolutely perfect.

Connor still held her other hand. Standing there in the middle of that quiet dirt road, surrounded by pine trees and hills, it felt like they were a family.

Chapter Fifteen
(in which Connor and Sadie dance)

Nearly two weeks later, Sadie pressed a palm to her stomach, scowling at the way the fluttering of her belly stirred anxiety throughout the rest of her body.

What am I doing?

Fine time to ask that question. She stretched herself straight and cleared her throat, meeting her own gaze in the mirror that stood in the corner of her childhood room. "It's a good plan. He'll be good to Reid." Her hands trembled, and a lump swelled in her throat.

This was her wedding day, and she wanted to crumple into a sobbing heap. Since that beautiful storybook moment on the road, she and Connor had only communicated through texts, a fact that reminded her with perfect clarity what this relationship really was. And wasn't. She clenched her fists and lifted her chin. Marriage wasn't always romance. Just read the Bible. So many marriages had come about because of an arrangement. A convenience. Or a necessity. This wasn't an immoral plan—quite the opposite.

I'm using him, taking advantage of his generosity fed by guilt. Lord, is that wrong? Of course it was. Only a pathetically flawed woman would even ask such a question. Or a desperate one. Sadie was undeniably both.

God forgive me, but I need him. Reid needs him. A hard ball of resentment formed. God knew the reason very well, and He could have prevented at least that much. Why would he let a single mother get sick like this? As soon as the haughty thought formed, ugly shame crept in. God owed her nothing. Absolutely nothing.

"Forgive me," she repeated, this time as a whisper to the empty space.

As if a response to her repentance, her phone chimed. Her shoulders slumped under her misery, she reached to the dresser and checked the text.

Connor. Her stomach twisted so hard she thought she'd be sick.

Good morning.

He was going to back out. Even with such an innocent text, she was sure Connor was going to tell her he couldn't go through with it. He'd had the past many days to really think this through and he'd come to the reasonable conclusion that this was crazy.

Then what would she do?

I should have said something sooner, but...

Lord, give her strength.

I don't know what to wear today.

Her lungs emptied with a whoosh as relief had her sagging against the bed. He wasn't backing out. Cradling the phone, she typed back with trembling fingers. *It doesn't matter. It's just a JP.*

It's our wedding day, Sadie. Your wedding day. Tell me what to wear.

Warm liquid lined her lids as she closed her eyes, from both gratitude and grief. No one *wanted* to marry this way. But his bold willingness soothed the frayed edges of her heart. More importantly, Connor was giving Reid hope for the future. A good, promising future.

Rising, Sadie walked to the closet she had, for the past two days, spent way too much time in front of, debating. The decision had been made last night. She had settled on a simple straight dark-brown skirt and a baby-blue wrap top. Hardly wedding-like, but she'd made up her mind it didn't matter. This arrangement was more like a business deal than a marriage anyway. Sort of.

With a warm rush of longing, Sadie let her gaze travel to the lovely dress she'd pulled out of its plastic bag. Cream chiffon overlay a sheath the lightest shade of lavender. The style was of an Audrey Hepburn nature, with the Sabrina neckline, the trim belted waist, and A-line skirt. At the collar, on the left side, a gathering of delicate Johnny-jump-ups had been embroidered, and a deep-purple satin belt completed the dress.

She'd loved it at first sight a little over a year ago when she'd spotted it on a rack at a thrift store, and though she had no reason to buy such an ensemble, she couldn't resist spending the fifteen dollars. It had gone from purchase to dry cleaning to her tiny apartment closet back in Carson City, and then from her packed bags to this closet without a real purpose. She'd never worn it. As Sadie fingered the tiny perfect flowers, a calm eased into her taut body, and her stomach settled.

The phone she'd left on the bed chimed again.

Sadie? At least tell me what color tie.

Connor was wearing a suit. Sadie lifted her eyes back to the dress, and the decision was made. *Purple, if you have it,* she typed. *Or gray.*

Thank you. See you soon?

Another long breath left her lungs, this time steady and much less painful. *Yes. I'll be there.*

***

Connor had to search his brothers' closets for the purple tie. He was more of a black-and-white man, but he'd asked Sadie, and he wanted her to be pleased. It was, after all, her wedding.

Inside the courthouse, he paced the marble tiled floor, adjusting his tie. He stopped at the glass-paneled door and scanned the slant parking spots, anxious to see a gray Jeep. Still no. With a flip of his wrist, he checked his watch. Not yet 0900. He had a habit of being early—and if Sadie was anything like she'd been in high school, she had a habit of being late.

She'll be here.

With a roll of his shoulders, Connor tried to work out the knots clumping at his neck. Dad and Mom would be there soon too. He'd asked them to lag a few minutes, to give him a few moments alone with Sadie before their appointment. If his bride didn't get there soon, however, that would be a bust.

His reflection gave him a momentary distraction, and he straightened the tie that had already been perfectly straight, fixed the hair that hadn't been out of place, and tugged on his perfectly placed jacket.

Come on, Sadie...

And there she was. All at once her Jeep pulled up to the recently plowed slot and parked, and the woman he was minutes away from calling his wife stepped out of the vehicle. With her head down, she clasped the front of her wool dress coat closed and jogged toward the building.

He opened the door for her. "Hi."

With a hesitant flick of her gaze up to him, she breathed a wavering response. "Hi."

She began to slip her arms from her coat sleeves, and he lifted it from her frame, hanging it up on the coat rack in the corner. When he turned back to her, he stopped short.

Connor's heart stalled with an electrified ache, and his breath caught as he let his gaze travel the length of her. Her honey-brown hair had been swept back and off her face, allowing him to freely take in the satin look of her skin, the elegant length of her neck, and slim build of her shoulders. She wore a dress of cream and purple that perfectly fit her feminine curves until it flared out at her waist. The gauzy material draped around her legs to her knees. On her feet, he found a pair of white canvas slip-on tennis shoes, which made him chuckle.

Stepping toward her, he found her face again. The purple of her dress made the blue of her eyes appear lavender, and his grin suddenly felt more captivated than amused. "You look stunning."

Her lips rolled together as she looked down. "I wasn't sure I should wear it. It's a summer dress and a little too fancy for this."

"For your wedding?"

He watched her shoulders move as she drew in a breath. "It's strange to think that's what this is."

Nervously, Connor reached to trace the bare skin of her arm, starting at her shoulder and following the length of it until he came to her fingers. There, he took her hand. "Are you sure,

Sadie?"

"That I want to do this?"

He nodded.

"Yes. I'm...I'm sure." With a pained look, she studied him a moment. "Are you?"

After the conversations he'd had with his parents and with Jackson, he was more determined, as if his reasons outlined for them had given him more confidence where he'd felt unsteady before. He and Sadie would make this work. For Reid, she would. For her and for her son—soon to be his as well—he would. Commitment would be their foundation. The security of Reid's future would be their course marker. It was honorable, and it was something he felt compelled to.

"Connor?"

His whispered name jolted him back to the moment, and he realized he'd been standing there with her hand in his, staring.

"It's not too late," she said.

With a half smile, he lifted her fingers to brush them against his lips. "I'm sure, Sadie." When her lovely eyes searched his again, he stepped closer, tucking her hand against his chest. "Quite sure."

The sound of car doors closing broke the sweet moment between them, and Connor looked over his shoulder to see both his parents and then hers approaching the courthouse. With his hand tucked safely in hers, Reid walked beside Mrs. Allen, his serious face tipped upward as he scanned the courthouse building.

Connor was acquiring a wife and a son, all in one day. Tender warmth moved in his heart as he watched the boy take the steps and then come through the door.

"Connor," Reid said, his face brightening. His short legs ran to him, and then the boy's arms flung around Connor's knees. "Today you marry us."

Connor chuckled as he knelt beside him. "I do." He tugged on the small suit coat that had lain beneath the winter coat Mrs. Allen had just tugged from the boy's arms. "You look very handsome, Airman."

Reid grinned and then gave him a stiff salute. "Reporting for duty, sir."

The group gathered around them laughed, and Connor was grateful for the ease of tension that had followed them into the foyer.

Mom stepped toward Sadie, a cloth bundle in her hand. Unease moved within Connor's chest as his mom reached toward the woman he was marrying.

"These are for you. A girl needs a bouquet on her wedding day." She unwrapped the white tea towel and passed a floral creation of white hydrangeas and evergreens. "I'm sorry. I didn't know your colors, so I just went with white."

A look of deep humility crossed Sadie's face before she worked up a small smile. "They're lovely. Thank you."

Tension drained from Connor's shoulders. He should have known better than to think Mom would be anything but kind to Sadie, even if she had expressed her reservations about this marriage.

"Murphy-Allen?" A woman rounded the office in front of the county courtroom, her heels clicking against the marble and echoing throughout the vaulted foyer.

Connor stood and strode toward Sadie. "That's us." He found her free hand and took it, her fingers cold in his grip.

"We're ready if you are," the woman said.

He looked to Sadie's face, finding it pale. But when she tipped her chin to meet his eyes, she nodded.

So then, here it was. Time to get married.

***

Connor was quiet as he drove. His posture, as ever, remained straight, his expression fixed in that unreadable neutrality. The road had been plowed clear of the six inches of snow the skies had dumped the night before, but the curves of the mountain highway still made Sadie nervous as they climbed their way out of town.

Sadie gripped the handful of flowers Connor's mom had given her before their little...ceremony? Had it been a ceremony? Her stomach rolled, and she wasn't sure if it was from the movement of the car or from the reality of what had just taken place.

Whatever it was called, it was done. Connor and she were now legally husband and wife.

In the midst of the deep discomfort that thought brought, a pair of memorable moments sent a rush of warmth through her veins, easing the nausea in her belly. When the judge had asked if they were exchanging rings, Connor had reached into his pocket, withdrawing a simple white-gold band.

"I-I don't have one for you," she'd stammered.

He'd taken her hand and winked, and she'd felt like she had that moment so many years back when he'd asked her to go to the winter formal. All fluttery and mushy and happy. "It's okay. I'll marry you anyway," he'd said.

And then, breaths later, Judge Stevens declared them husband and wife. There had been an uncertain lull, an acutely uncomfortable beat in which no one seemed to know what to do next.

"You can kiss your wife, if you want, Mr. Murphy," the judge said, a teasing tone in her voice.

Sadie's attention flew to Connor, finding his gaze already settled on her. The tenderness he held on her melted her like butter. He leaned nearer and whispered, "May I?"

Suddenly, all she wanted was to experience his kiss. A girlish reaction, one full of fancifully romantic ideas, but one that she didn't bat away. "Yes," she'd breathed.

The tips of his fingers traced the line of her jaw, tilting her mouth to his, and then the pad of his thumb smoothed over her cheekbone a breath before his lips brushed over hers.

It had been a butterfly-soft touch. Merely a tickling pass of his mouth on hers. But it had made her belly tighten and a delicious electric pulse spark through her veins. Even as she sat there in the awkward silence of the car ride back to her parents' house, the simple memory of it sent a fresh current through her all over again.

The car slowed, and Sadie realized she'd closed her eyes as those moments replayed. As the momentum of their travel pushed right, she regathered her senses.

This wasn't the turn to her parents', where her mother would be laying out a brunch for the small wedding party.

"Where are we going?"

Connor glanced at her and then put his attention back on the hill he'd turned down. "I thought maybe we could take a little time to ourselves. Do you remember the riverbend picnic spot?"

"Yes." Everyone in Sugar Pine remembered the picnic spot. The nearby lower falls would thunder in the springtime, and the glen near the calmer stretch of water was a favorite for picnicking and fishing. Among the high school crowd, it was a favorite spot for other reasons as well.

Heat rushed over her, and she was certain her cheeks flushed crimson.

They crossed the bridge over the ice-edged river and then turned into the parking area. Once he had the car stopped, Connor peeked at her again and clearly noticed the change in her color.

"Don't—I mean, that's not why." He cleared his throat. "I got takeout from the Storm Café. Pancakes, and those vanilla cherries you like. I asked your mom and dad if they'd take Reid for a while. Just so you and I can have a bit of time to talk. To...adjust."

She had no idea what to say.

"I'm sorry. I should have asked you first." He leaned forward to start the car again.

"It's okay." Her words came out in a rush.

Hand hovering over the keys, Connor looked at her again. How could a grown man—a seasoned military man—look that uncertain? Especially one as confident and as purposeful as Connor Murphy? But as his lips pressed together and his brows folded inward, he looked more and more like he was lost and afraid.

"It was a nice idea," she said.

He studied her, and then his gaze moved to the scene beyond the car. "I didn't think about the snow. Or that you would be wearing a dress. Or that this would seem like...like a...a setup or something." His hand fell to his thigh, as did his attention.

The ring on her left hand caught a flicker of morning sunlight as it flashed through the evergreen trees. Sadie sighed as she pressed against the backrest of the seat. "The food was thoughtful of you."

"Are you hungry?"

"No, not really."

Connor exhaled. So far, day one of marriage was not going smoothly. She rolled her empty hand into a fist and searched her mind for something to say.

"It's not really what you dreamed of as a girl when you thought about your wedding day, is it?" His tone sounded...sorry. As if this was his fault.

Sadie unlatched her seat belt and leaned forward to place her bouquet on the dashboard. He shouldn't feel bad. "There's not much about my life that looks like what I used to imagine."

With a tentative move, Connor reached for her hand. When he took it, his hold was gentle. "I'm sorry, Sadie."

He'd be sorry for everything for the rest of his life. Of that, she was certain. That was the reason he'd done this, that he'd agreed to marry her. It made her feel grateful and wretched all at once.

His thumb ran over her knuckles, and then he wove her fingers into his. "Is there something about your wedding that you really wanted? Something maybe we could do?"

So sweet. The gesture made her hurt.

"No. No there's nothing." She stared at the lacing of their fingers, his curling over hers, his warm hand swallowing her cold one. He'd given her his ring, his name, and his life. She had no right to want more.

Squeezing his hand, she moved her gaze to find his eyes again. "What about you? Is there something you hoped to do at your wedding?"

His lips met again, the unreadable, neutral expression modeling his features.

"Connor?" she pressed.

Surprisingly, a tint of red brushed over his cheeks. There was something.

"Tell me."

"It's silly," he said.

"It's your wedding."

"Our wedding."

"Okay. Our wedding. Tell me what you would have wanted."

"I-I had always looked forward to the first introduction. You know, when they say, 'Ladies and gentlemen, welcome for the first time Mr. and Mrs. Connor Murphy.' And then we would have our first dance."

She stared at him, stunned. One, because she was now Mrs. Connor Murphy. That hadn't hit her yet, but to hear him say it was...crazy. Beautiful crazy, if she was being honest. And second, because she had no idea something like a first introduction and dance would matter to driven, direct, and honor-bound Connor Murphy.

But it did.

Unlacing her fingers from his, she fished in her coat for her phone.

"What are you doing?" he asked.

"Hold on." She searched her play lists, found the soundtrack for *Jekyll and Hyde,* the musical, and pulled up "Someone Like You," and then she popped open her door.

"Sadie, there's six inches of fresh snow out there."

"The parking lot is plowed, and I wore tennis shoes."

At that, he laughed.

"Come on." She waved him out of the car and set her phone on the hood. When he stood in front of her, she pressed Play and took his hand.

He stood still for a moment, just taking her in with that tender look that had melted her at the courthouse. And then she was in his arms, swaying to the music.

"Ladies and gentlemen..." His hold tightened around her, and his deep murmuring voice sent thrilling waves down her neck and back. "Please welcome for the first time Mr. and Mrs. Connor

Murphy."

He fell quiet as she pressed her forehead against him. There, in the fresh snow with only the trees to witness, they shared their first dance as husband and wife. Sadie was certain the beauty of it was more than she deserved.

Chapter Sixteen

(in which everything is different)

"I don't like broccoli!"

Connor heard Reid's building fit from behind the closed bedroom door. Honestly, it'd been a day already. A near miss at the tower—the resulting paperwork for it equaled approximately the same amount required for a volume of *War and Peace*, not to mention piling exhaustion. He'd called Sadie when it had been near six o'clock and told her he'd be late. She'd sounded every bit as tired, and he couldn't blame her.

In the two weeks he'd spent as a married man, he'd barely slept, and not for typical groom reasons. He and Sadie shared a room—and a bed, but he'd been diligent about giving her space. Making sure she had all the privacy she needed because obviously they weren't anywhere near a typical newlywed couple. The whole setup—and the sense of being wrung out and run down—made him wonder how Jackson had survived his first year of marriage.

His brother had warned him that this would be hard. Harder than Connor had imagined. Connor hadn't banked on how awkward it all would be. Maybe he'd believed that it'd just be like the barracks or like having a roommate again? Being married was most certainly not like that at all. And on top of the sheer awkwardness of the adjustment, there was the high-volt trepidation about Sadie's upcoming radical hysterectomy, after which her full radiation and chemo treatments would ensue. All of it had them both on a razor-sharp edge.

Bottom line: Connor was in way, way over his head.

"No!" Reid shouted this time. "I hate it! You're a mean mommy!"

The sigh that vibrated Connor's chest was something between a groan and a growl. Yanking a clean T-shirt on and tossing his BDUs toward the hamper, he opened the bedroom door and marched down the hall.

Honeymoon was over then. Such as it was. He and Reid had been doing really well—the kid sort of worshiped him, so that had helped initially. But this... Nuh-uh. Not letting it pass.

"Reid." His tone was a sharp demand, something he might have used if he'd been a drill sergeant at basics at any point in his career.

That little blond head whipped around, wide, startled eyes pointed up at him. Sadie also turned to him, her lips pressed hard. She eyed him warily and gave a slight shake of her head. Connor met her silent warning with one of his own. He wasn't tolerating a disrespectful boy in his home. Not now, not ever. If she weren't so tired and emotionally wrung out, Sadie wouldn't be having it either, of that Connor was certain.

When he shifted his attention back to Reid, his irritation moved rapidly toward anger. Broccoli florets were scattered over the table and floor around Reid's chair, his plate overturned in a telling position.

"Did you throw that?" He pointed to the mess.

Reid scowled, but his bottom lip trembled. "I don't like them," he whispered with deflating defiance.

"Doesn't matter. You can't treat your mother that way."

His little chin lifted. "She's mean!"

Connor moved forward, his reach targeting Reid.

Sadie gripped his elbow as he passed her. "I can handle my son," she whispered.

"Nope." He glanced toward her at his shoulder and then refocused on Reid. "That won't fly, young man." The moment his hands lifted the boy, Reid exploded into a full-fledged fit. Kicking. Yelling. Tears.

"I don't wanna! I not gonna! I don't like you, Connor! You mean... you mean... you mean..."

Every sobbed shout pierced Connor's heart while at the same time winding up his frustration. *He's just a kid. This is just a tantrum...* Growing up as one of the older siblings of seven boys, he knew a fit when he saw one. Connor kept his mouth shut, reminding himself that kids weren't always rational as he struggled to grip a calm he didn't feel. He walked the flailing boy to Reid's bedroom and set him down on the new bedspread they'd all picked out and bought together the day Sadie and Reid moved in.

Firmly, he held Reid's sides and squatted in front of him. "You won't do that here. Or anywhere else. Your mother deserves your respect, and you will learn self-control."

"You're not the boss of me!"

Connor flinched, as if that little foot that had just slammed into his chest actually hurt. How could a four-year-old's words punch that hard? "Reid, you're going to sit in here by yourself until you can be calm and respectful." Drawing a breath, he stood and strode back out the way he came, ignoring Reid's wild protests. Once out of the room, he pulled the door shut, keeping his fist on the knob, and leaned back against the frame.

"I was handling it," Sadie hissed. She stepped into the space across from him, her arms crossed, chin edged up at him—the exact defiant look Reid had shot Connor's way moments before.

Hot anger rolled through his veins, and Connor leaned forward, nearly giving vent to the building steam. By some miracle, he pinned his mouth shut and simply shook his head. Sadie dropped her eyes, which were sheened, and moved toward the other door at the end of the hall. Once through, she shut it, leaving Connor alone in the dim hallway, listening to Reid's mellowing cries and wondering if his wife had just locked him out of his bedroom for the night.

What had she expected him to do? Ignore the boy he was claiming as his son while the kid threw broccoli at her?

Not happening. And he felt completely blindsided by her anger about it. How was he supposed to navigate instant fatherhood if Sadie wasn't going to back him?

The back of his head bumped against the doorframe as he shut his eyes. *God, help me. Help us.* What had he been thinking, assuming he could be Reid's dad? Imagining that going from the beloved *Mr. Sergeant Connor* to *Daddy* would be smooth sailing?

Confidence falling apart, Connor surrendered to prayer. He had no idea what else to do.

***

Sitting cross-legged on the bed she was still trying to reconcile as being hers—hers and *Connor's*—Sadie stared at the wall separating their room from Reid's. Though her eyes burned, there were no tears. She was too mad for tears.

Fingers rolled into fists, she swallowed against the urge to stomp back out into that hall and lay into Connor. Who did he think he was anyway, handling her son like that? It wasn't his place to step in. He'd scared Reid, picking the boy up like that and hauling him off to his room.

She should have done it, and long before Connor had stormed out of the bedroom. If only she hadn't been so tired, if only she'd been practicing better motherhood.

A piercing sense of failure knifed into her. She wasn't a good mom. Look what she'd gotten herself and Reid into. What if Connor was the sort of man who would lose his temper and hurt Reid?

Clearly he isn't.

Involuntary images of Connor and Reid playing with the Hot Wheels track, building Legos, and playfully wrestling during the evenings the past several days flooded her mind. Connor was smitten with her son—something that provoked a curious...jealousy?...in her heart. Why, she couldn't say; she was pleased that the pair had bonded so beautifully. But yes, envy was there. And she should have learned from past mistakes where envy led.

Connor adores Reid.

The calm voice of reason spoke into her mounting outrage.

Why, exactly, was she so mad at Connor? He'd stepped in, defending her, requiring Reid's respect for her. Was that really so criminal?

On the other side of that wall, Reid's cries lessened and then muffled into nothing. The scruff of a door scraping against carpet sounded, but not from the room she was in. Connor was going back into Reid's room.

"Are you ready to talk?" Connor's low voice held distinct authority.

Sadie squeezed her eyes shut, imagining Reid staring up at the man she'd married with fear etched into his little face. She couldn't handle that vision. Her little boy had never had a consistent male authority figure in his life—Reid wouldn't know what to do with it. Pressing her sock-covered feet to the carpet, she went to her door, opened it, and crept the few feet down the hall until she could see into Reid's room.

Shoulders rounded, hands on either side of Reid against the bed, Connor was on his knees in front of her son. Reid's face was puffy red and streaked with tears, but there wasn't fear in his expression. He shook his head, holding Connor's gaze.

"I don't like broccoli," the boy whispered again.

"I get that. But that doesn't make it okay for you to yell at your mom or to throw your plate. That's not okay, Reid."

Bottom lip trembling, Reid looked down as he rolled his little hands together in his lap. Connor used his thick index finger to lift Reid's chin. "It's not okay, buddy," he repeated. "It's not how good men behave, and you will say sorry to your mom for being disrespectful and ugly."

A big ol' crocodile tear seeped from Reid's brown eyes and rolled down his cheek. Connor caught it with his thumb and wiped it away.

"Sorry, Connor," Reid sputtered.

Without hesitation, Connor had her boy hauled up against his chest, making Sadie's heart shatter and mending it all in one swoop.

"Daddy, remember?" Connor's deep voice wobbled, like he

might be barely holding himself together too.

Reid shifted back to look up at Connor again. "You'll still be my daddy?"

"I'm always gonna be your daddy now, Reid. It's for keeps."

A pair of little arms circled around Connor's neck, followed by a set of scrawny legs around his chest. The muscles in Connor's shoulders strained against his T-shirt as he lifted Reid against him.

"You're forgiven, Reid. Let's go make it right with Mom now, okay?"

Sadie scooted away from the door as Connor moved to stand.

"Then you have some cleaning up to do, got it?" she heard Connor continue while she retreated into their bedroom.

She didn't hear Reid's answer. And he mustn't have given one to Connor, because then she heard, "How about a *yes, sir*, or *yes, Dad*" from Connor.

Don't push it, Connor, Sadie thought, a hint of resentment swirling in her mind.

"Yes, Daddy," Reid said, his voice regaining confidence.

Huh. How did that work?

She wasn't given more time to ponder it, because Connor filled the doorway, Reid in his arms. Stopping just past the entry, he whispered something in Reid's ear and then set him onto the carpet, giving his shoulder a squeeze after he was steady on his feet.

Reid's look was all remorse, making her mother's heart achy and soft. Sadie held out a hand to him, and he moved toward her until he was at her knees beside the bed.

"I'm sorry, Mommy."

"It's okay, Reid. I forgot you don't like broccoli."

"He can eat a little broccoli; it won't kill him." Connor's interjection ripped Reid's attention from her face to his, and Sadie looked up with a mighty scowl. He lifted a brow, unmistakably at her first and then directed his look back to Reid. "Will it, Reid?"

Her son shuffled uncomfortably, looking at his feet. "But I

don't like it."

"There are things in life we don't like, buddy. But it just takes a few minutes of being strong to get them done. You can do that."

Again, Reid hesitated, and then he nodded. "Okay."

"Good boy." Connor held out his hand, and Reid went to him easily enough. Together, the pair strode from the room.

Sadie sat alone again, resenting Connor as much as she appreciated him while she heard the two of them cleaning up the mess.

***

Connor stared at the coffee table while he prayed silently for wisdom. He felt too tired, and honestly too frustrated, to go in and talk to Sadie. But there had been a phrase his dad had pounded into him—into all the Murphy boys—that wouldn't leave his mind in peace.

Sleeping mad on a fight will only lead to you waking up mad and ready for more.

He scanned the past few hours in his memory, trying to pinpoint exactly why Sadie would draw out this angry silence. Did she really want him to just act like a passive roommate? Stay out of her and Reid's world, out of their struggles? Is that what she thought this marriage would look like?

Sadie had said at one point that she wanted Reid to have a father. Did she really want Connor to be only fun-guy dad? Never-discipline-the-boy dad? Silent stepdad? Man, they should have discussed this before, because he couldn't be that guy. It just wasn't in him, and he really believed that approach wouldn't be the best thing for Reid.

This was just an adjustment thing. All of them needed time and grace to adjust. *Please, God, let that be true.* Connor continued to beg for a reality that looked a lot different than this, because a continual life of silent resentment and struggle didn't match with what he'd imagined for all of them.

Connor snatched his phone from the coffee table and ran a quick line to Jackson. *You weren't kidding about the hard thing.*

Jackson must have been near his phone, because his response

came quick. *No, brother, I wasn't. Bad day?*

Yeah.

Praying for you.

Thanks.

No advice, but somehow Connor felt a bit of stability sink into his spirit. Silence filled the apartment, so much more uncomfortable than it had ever felt when it was him on his own. Well then, it was up to him to bridge the gap, to seek reconciliation. He guessed.

"Pray hard, Jackson," Connor muttered as he stood. "I have no experience with this."

Maybe if he had dated more after high school. Connor hadn't—he'd been too scared he would screw up someone else's life. Knowing how much he'd messed up Sadie's world kept him to himself, for the most part, when it came to relationships with women. In the years since high school, Connor could count on two hands the number of dates he'd actually gone on, most of those being coerced setups. He didn't even need a hand to number the steady girlfriends he'd had since then, as that grand total had been zero. Which meant he had zero practice at this making-up-after-a-fight thing.

He sorted through where he should begin as he went to the kitchen for a drink of water—delaying his trek to the bedroom. An apology was always a good start, wasn't it? Except he wasn't sorry. He didn't believe he'd done anything wrong.

Back to the cold silence thing again, then. Why was Sadie being unreasonable? Would she tell him if he asked?

Probably not if he said it like that.

Lord, wisdom!

Were all marriages a setup to see how inept a man was? How desperately he needed more than what he had?

Connor blew out a frustrated breath and forced himself to face the chilly woman who had gone to bed well over an hour before. Maybe he'd find her asleep. Again, his dad's words seeped through his mind. Yeah, that'd be no good if Sadie was asleep.

With a heavy sense of dread, Connor eased the bedroom door open. The room was dark, but enough of the city lights filtered through the cracks of the shaded window that he could make out her profile. Face tipped to the ceiling, she lay stiff, which led him to believe that she was not asleep.

He'd seen her sleep—she was soft and approachable, and having her beside him in his bed had been a thing of longing from day one. She smelled sweet and gave a warmth that blankets couldn't offer, and her distinct womanly form had made it impossible for him to imagine this was a *roommate* situation. He longed to have her fill his arms, to hold all that soft beauty that was Sadie close.

Too bad this wasn't that kind of marriage.

"Sadie." He spoke softly as he lowered onto the mattress, sitting next to her on her side of the bed.

Only the slightest turn of her chin indicated she heard him. Connor brushed away the temptation to be irritated, call it a night, and let her have her silent way about this. *Be quick to listen, slow to speak, and slow to become angry.*

The verse from James, one that Mom had given all her boys on multiple occasions, came as a rescue line and a guidepost marking this unknown territory. It also provoked another question: *How would I treat her if she were the love of my life?* Seemed like an odd thing to ask about the woman who was his wife.

Hesitantly, Connor reached for the outline of her face, feathering his fingers along her skin. At her hairline near her ears, he found a telling dampness.

"Sadie, let's not end the day like this."

She sniffed.

He still didn't understand her reaction, but this made his heart softer, less frustrated. Leaning, he reached for the bedside lamp and flicked it on. The moment his sight connected with her eyes, he wished he'd left the room dark. Anger hardened her look, even with the tears.

Defensiveness rose up strong. "I would never hurt Reid, Sadie. You have to know that."

"He was scared of you."

"He was scared of being in trouble—which he probably should worry about. Did you think I should let him yell and throw things at my wife?"

She flinched, and a softness eased her mouth. "He's only four, Connor."

At her quieter tone, Connor felt the tension in his shoulders lessening. "I know that." He took her hand. "And I swear I won't hurt him. But little boys don't just grow out of being selfish and disrespectful. They don't just suddenly figure out on their own how to be kind and polite and good. They have to be taught these things."

"So you've been a dad for two weeks and suddenly you're an expert?"

Her sharp tone and harsh words had him sitting back, clenching his jaw. Releasing her hand, he turned so he faced the wall rather than her and sighed. "You want me to stay out of it? Watch you struggle with Reid and do nothing?"

Sadie sniffed again.

"How can you expect that from me, Sadie?"

Her muffled breath told him she was crying. He wished he knew why. Was she only mad? Did she regret everything about them? What did she want from him? He turned back to her. "I need you to talk to me. We're married—it's done. I need you to help me figure out how to do this. Do you really want me to do nothing when Reid is misbehaving?"

"No," she said on a cry. "But I don't like feeling like I'm a bad mother."

"What?"

"I hate that you saw him that way. I hate that you saw me that way...and now you think that I can't handle my son."

Without a second thought, Connor reached for her. "Sadie." She sat up willingly, and suddenly she was huddled against his chest, filling his arms.

He felt a few layers that had been the barrier between them fall.

We'll be okay... Squeezing his eyes shut, he leaned his cheek against her head. "Reid's a great kid. You're a good mom, Sadie. I've never thought otherwise. I promise."

Her shoulders moved as she let emotion spill out. "I feel like I have to give him up."

"That's not true at all. I'm not taking him away, Sadie. That was never what this was."

"I know. I just don't know how to share—it's always been Reid and me."

Connor rubbed small circles into one shoulder with his thumb, and his other hand cradled her head. "I get it," he whispered.

"I'm sorry, Connor."

As she snaked her arms around him, the rest of his frustration drained away. He pressed a kiss to her head. "We'll figure this out."

He hoped. Prayed. They needed to—this was life now. And though he felt less certain about this path than he had two weeks before, he wasn't going back on his word. He wanted this new reality to be good for all of them.

Chapter Seventeen

(in which Sadie goes to the hospital)

Connor squeezed his hands together. Waiting had never been this hard. At the warm touch on his shoulder, he looked up. Compassion filled Dad's eyes as he held Connor's look. As if tracing the same thoughts, they both turned toward the Allens, sitting across the waiting room.

"How are you holding up, Mrs. Allen?" Connor's voice felt unstable as he spoke into the tense silence.

Sadie's mom gave him a wobbly smile. "Just Eleanor is fine, Connor. Maybe someday even Mom?"

He forced the corners of his mouth to lift and nodded. He was still grappling with being married. Calling his mother-in-law, who had been *Mrs. Allen* to him ever since he could remember, *Mom* felt like a leap too far to make.

"I'm okay," she said. Mr. Allen's hand covered Eleanor's as she spoke, and her brave front crumpled. "No, that's not true at all. I am at once praying that the surgery will be successful and that they'll get all the cancer, while lamenting that Sadie will never have the chance to carry another baby. It's a heartbreaking thing for a mother to face—especially because we dealt with years of infertility. I remember keenly that pain."

Husband and wife huddled together, and Connor detected a tear or two from Mr. Allen, making it even more difficult for him to keep his own rocking emotions in place. The reality was now out there, spoken out loud. No matter what direction this marriage took, Sadie would never carry his child.

He'd been okay with that. Though he'd grown up in a bursting house of many kids, having only one son hadn't been a deal to him before. But there, sitting in the surgery waiting room while doctors removed the bulk of his wife's reproductive system, the fresh reminder of that reality stung.

This was his choice though. He'd made it with full disclosure, willingly. And though he felt a surge of pain that took him by surprise in that moment, he didn't feel regret. Not for his choice.

Connor stood, glanced at his dad for the silent strength he knew he could count on, and then stepped to the seat beside Mrs. Allen. "I'm thankful for Reid."

She took his hand with a mighty grip. "I feel like you've given up something precious for my daughter, and I'm not sure what to do with that."

"Don't." He covered her fingers. "I have a family because of her, and I'm grateful." It was an honest statement—one that rang truer than he'd realized before he'd said it. He loved Reid, all the way down into the deepest places of his heart, and truly claiming him as his son wasn't hard at all. And Sadie...

God, please make her well.

In that moment he realized, with sudden clarity and strength, that he wanted a life with her. One that was more than a deal birthed from duty. He wanted a life of partnership and joy. And love.

Can we have that? Will You give us that chance, Lord?

A woman in scrubs pushed through the door separating the OR from the waiting room. "Mr. Murphy?"

"Yes." Connor glanced at Mr. and Mrs. Allen before he stood. They nodded, and she released his hand.

"Your wife is in recovery."

"Is she okay?"

"Everything went as well as could be hoped for." The surgeon, whom Connor had met before, held his eyes with a serious but hopeful look. "I want to keep her for observation and pain management for a few days."

Connor nodded. They had discussed this at the pre-op

appointment a few days before. He and Sadie had had another awkward discussion following that appointment. He'd put in for leave for those days she would be in the hospital. She hadn't wanted him to. *My parents are coming. They can keep Reid. They can make sure I'm okay once I'm out of the hospital. In fact, maybe I should just go back home with them until I've recovered...*

Until it finally became clear to him that she felt bad he was doing the things he did for her, he'd been upset that she seemed to be pushing him to the fringes of her life with her alternative plans.

They waded through the thick, murky swamp of guilt-driven plans, and after over a day's worth of discussion—much of which had been heated—they'd found a middle ground. He would take a couple leave days after she was out of the hospital. After they'd waded through and found a compromise, she'd filled the hollow space between his arms. A space that, standing there in the waiting room in that precarious moment, felt chilled and empty.

"You can go back, if you'd like," the doctor said. "She should be waking up soon."

He looked back at Sadie's parents.

"Go ahead, son," Mr. Allen said.

"You sure? I—"

"We'll wait." Mrs. Allen lifted another wobbly smile. "You can come get us when she's ready."

Nodding but feeling bad about it, Connor looked to his dad for help. Dad dipped one short nod. "I'll call your mom so she can tell Reid that Sadie is out of surgery, and then I'll go join them. Just send me some text updates. I'm guessing we'll be at the park or something."

Suddenly Connor felt like the world was too heavy. He needed to see Sadie. Wanted to hold Reid. More, he wanted all of this to go away, wanted for Sadie to be healthy and fine, for the three of them to be perfectly settled and happy, and to see the future as full of possibilities.

As if reading his emotional collapse, Dad stepped toward him and pulled him into a bear hug. Connor gripped him hard.

"God's strength, son." Then Dad released him, and Connor turned toward the waiting doctor, his whole heart set on seeing his wife.

***

Sadie folded her fingers around the beefy ones that covered her hand. Warm and strong, the touch lent her reassurance and strength even before she fluttered her eyelids open. In response to her grip, that hand lifted hers, and then the warmth of breath filled her palm, followed by the tenderness of a kiss.

At that, she did force her eyes open. Past the light that felt overwhelmingly intrusive and the blur of hard sleep, she found Connor. Gentle concern filled his eyes as he leaned down to her, still holding her hand. He pressed his lips against her forehead.

"How are you?" he murmured.

Shutting her eyes, Sadie took in the moment that seemed intimate and loving. Then she took inventory of herself. Her body felt heavy, but for the moment, there was no pain.

As Connor leaned back again, she sought those green eyes. "I'm okay," she said.

"Are you in pain?"

"Not yet." As she spoke, the truth of what had been taken from her landed hard on her heart. Without permission, a sudden tear slipped from the corner of her eye.

Raw emotion passed over Connor's expression as he reached to catch the running tear against his knuckles.

"I'm sorry," Sadie whispered.

"Why are you sorry? You're the one lying in a hospital bed. I'm sorry you're going through this."

Her lips quivered. Why was this man here? Two months ago he'd had no obligation to her. And what he had now, he'd volunteered for. Seemed like he'd given up so much to gain so little. "Why did you do this?"

With his thumb, he traced her eyebrow, and then he cradled her face in his palm. It took several breaths before he whispered an answer. When he finally did, it was with a choked voice. "I believe it's what God wants for me. For us."

Sadie flinched and looked away. God's will was for Connor to sacrifice his chance at love and family? For him to live his life out of duty? That seemed awfully hard, and it made her feel terrible.

"Sadie, whatever you're thinking right now, I don't think it's true."

She searched for beauty in the dormant, late-winter landscape outside the window in her room. To her eyes, it wasn't there. There was simply the bleakness of brown lifelessness—and the view felt terribly familiar to her heart. "How would you know that, when you don't know what I'm thinking?"

"You're scowling. Looking angry."

"I'm not angry—not at you." She turned to look at him again.

"I'm not unhappy." Connor moved from the chair that he'd slid to her bedside and lowered onto the mattress beside her. "I'm not thrilled to see you here like this, but I don't regret our marriage."

"Do you always make it a priority to say and do the right thing?" Unexpected bitterness surged in her tone.

Connor's brows pinched, and he studied her as if trying to trace her thoughts. "You know I don't."

Closing her eyes again, Sadie sighed, attempting to push away the ugly resentment that had rolled over her. How could she resent a man who had given her his life the way Connor had? No, that wasn't it; she didn't resent him. But there was a longing that hurt.

"I'm sorry. I can't think straight right now."

Again, he leaned to her, and this time he slipped his hands around her head and shoulders, snuggling her close to his chest. "Understandable."

For a time, she pressed her forehead into him, savoring the feel of being held. Comforted. If she tried really hard, she could make believe it was the same thing as being wanted and loved.

"Connor?"

"Yeah."

Needing something to hold, she fisted the sides of his T-shirt. "I'm afraid."

"Of what, hon?"

"This is going to get harder." Every part of life was going to be more difficult. The treatments that she would begin as soon as her body healed enough to handle them. And their marriage. His life. While she knew she didn't have his love, she certainly didn't want his resentment, but that felt like a very real possibility.

His hold around her strengthened, and he pressed a kiss to her hair. "I've got you, Sadie."

No, he was stuck with her, which was a deep root of her fears. How could a man love a life—a woman—with whom he felt trapped? Lying there in the security of his arms, that question mattered more than it ever had.

Because a truth became startlingly clear, that painful longing defined. Connor's devotion driven by honor and duty weren't enough. Maybe it was for him—she wasn't sure. But it wasn't enough for her. Selfish as it was, Sadie wanted his love.

***

Connor passed from the chilly late March air into the hospital lobby. After checking in as a visitor, a process he was now familiar with, he directed his steps to the second hall on the right, toward room 115.

It'd been a long four days. Sadie's recovery was slow, and she was battling some sort of infection, so that didn't help. Also, the lab reports that came back about the lymph nodes that the surgeon had removed along with the radical hysterectomy had not been encouraging. While it had been suspected to be so, hearing that the cancer cells had spread had been a hard blow. The most aggressive treatment of chemo and radiation would be required, and then...

Connor cut off that trail of thought. He needed to focus on now. The next step—and that was getting Sadie home and settled, helping her with the antibiotics that she'd self-administer through a PICC line that had been placed the day before, and focusing on getting her ready for the next step in treatment.

Not to mention finishing his air force career in the coming six weeks left in his contract. Then there was the whole figuring out what to do beyond that, especially since he now had a family to take care of.

His shoulders drooped.

"Mr. Murphy, can I have a word with you?"

Connor stopped a few feet short of Sadie's hospital room door, his attention piqued by the woman in scrubs in front of him. "Sure. Is it about Sadie?"

"Yes." Her hand gripped his arm, and then she tipped her head in a silent invitation to step into another room. Once there, she began again. "I'm Crystal. I've been your wife's nurse overnight."

He would have guessed that. Connor nodded, but concern knotted his gut. As of yet he hadn't been pulled aside by a medical professional to discuss Sadie. Everything had been out there in front of them together. "Everything go okay? I didn't get a call, and I thought Sadie was being discharged today."

"Yes, that's still the plan. And for the most part, your wife is doing well. But..." The middle-aged nurse gave him a look of hesitation, and maybe of compassion, and then plunged forward. "I'm stepping past my professional boundaries here, Mr. Murphy, but I feel like it's needed. You see, last night Sadie had an accident in bed that her protective clothing didn't absorb. She said it's not the first time that's happened, and that's not unusual with her condition. But she sort of lost it. Through her tears, she shared that you're recently married, and she's horrified to think this could happen at home." The rush of words stopped there, and that expression of hesitation morphed into pleading.

A sharp pain sliced through Connor's chest as he imagined Sadie's breakdown and her fears of embarrassment in front of him. He wanted to sit down and cry for her and to have a conversation with God about how this seemed terribly unfair. Instead, he swallowed and nodded. "I understand."

"Mr. Murphy, I really hope you do. I hope you understand that this isn't something she has control of."

"I do."

"Be gentle with her if—no, more likely, when—it happens at home. It's terribly humiliating."

Had she thought he would be cruel? How much detail regarding their recent marriage had Sadie shared with this woman? "Of course."

As Crystal looked toward the floor, her cheeks flushed. She began to step away, and then stopped, looking back up at him. "I'm so sorry you have to begin your life together this way. For both of you, I'm sorry. I'm sure it's not what you dreamed of."

He hadn't dreamed of a married life much at all since high school, but that likely wasn't what she meant. "Thank you." Connor didn't know what else could be said. "We'll pray our way through it, and I would never intentionally degrade my wife."

Stepping from the room and back into the hall, Crystal walked with him the short distance to Sadie's door. "I'll be in after a while to check her vitals. I think the doctor will be around within the hour. She should be released by noon."

Connor nodded again, and Crystal walked away. For many moments he remained planted outside the closed door, head down, heart breaking, praying. He had no compass for this. No way to know what to say, what to expect, how to navigate through the rough space ahead. As he prayed, he remembered what he'd told Sadie after she'd come out of surgery—that he'd done this because he had believed it was God's will.

He still believed that, even if he was realizing this life would be harder than he'd imagined.

With a fortifying breath and a final plea for wisdom, Connor pushed through the door. Sadie lay propped up in the bed, reading the Bible spread open in her lap. At his entry, she looked up. Her smile was wispy, and her tired eyes connected with his for only a moment.

"Hi." He strode to her bedside with more confidence than he felt and bent to kiss her head. Though he'd done this every day since her surgery, it still felt sadly awkward. Even so, he lingered over her, inhaling the scent of her. Her hair had lost the fresh scent of shampoo, and as his fingers slid into the mass of the braid that had come largely undone, he felt the oily grittiness that he felt certain she'd rather have washed away. Still, his heart moved at the privilege of touching her, at the intimacy of being so near. The grittier side of marriage, though rarely spoken of and even more seldomly celebrated, seemed a beautiful honor. He laid a cheek against the top of her head. "What are you reading this morning?"

Sadie lifted a hand, and the tips of her fingers traced the length of his arm. The simple act of her receiving him that way filled him with an unexpected hope. Her hand dropped, however, and she tipped away from him. "Genesis. I wanted to see the beauty of creation as God first made it."

Connor stood, repositioned a chair beside her bed, and lowered onto it. He looked at the Bible spread open on her lap, thinking about the first marriage. Remembering how before the first disobedience of man, Adam and Eve lived together without shame, image bearers of God, content in the dignity He gave them.

He wondered if, after the fall of man, marriage became a step toward restoration—that together he and Sadie would honor that God-given dignity in each other, and in doing so they would honor what God had intended from the beginning.

Overwhelmed by that idea and by the emotion wrought over the last few days, Connor reached to cover Sadie's hand, which rested against the blankets.

As if sensing the direction of his thoughts and not wanting to delve them, Sadie looked at him with a forced brightness. "How's Reid this morning?"

"He's good." Connor settled more comfortably on the chair. "I dropped him off with the grandparents before I came here."

"My parents or yours?"

"Yours, but I think they were planning to meet mine for breakfast at an IHOP or something, and then they're all off to do something fun again."

Sadie's small laugh sounded genuine; her smile seemed less waxy. "He's going to be spoiled before I make it home. As if he didn't get grandparentized enough with my parents, now he has yours going full-force spoilage on him too."

That made Connor chuckle. Though both Dad and Mom had expressed their concerns for his and Sadie's decision to marry, now that they were, they'd embraced Reid as their grandson, no holding back. Though it shouldn't have surprised him, watching them dump grandparent-level affection on Reid brought a tremendous amount of relief to Connor.

"He's having a ball—but he does miss his mom." He squeezed Sadie's hand. "Asked last night after we read a couple stories when you would come home and then clapped his hands when I told him that it'd be today."

A mist hazed Sadie's eyes. "Thank you for taking care of him."

Connor wanted to say no thanks needed, that Reid was his son now too, even if the state hadn't recognized it yet. But he held back.

Sadie tipped her chin and searched his face, an earnestness in her eyes drawing Connor's heart nearer the surface. Man, if she looked at him like that more often... Made him think that the growing want for her true affection wasn't just a flimsy wish.

"You're a good father, Connor."

Their parenting fight the week before her surgery floated back to the surface of his mind, making her compliment mean even more than it would, which was quite a lot to begin with. Connor lifted her hand and grazed a kiss across her knuckles. "You've given me a fine boy to work with, Sadie. Thank you for sharing him with me."

The tightness around her eyes hinted that she had thought of that fight as well. This marriage thing—and parenting thing—it was work. But they were working, and these kinds of hard but good moments were encouraging.

Thinking of hard moments... Connor tucked Sadie's hand against his chest and leaned forward. "I hear you had a rough night last night."

By the flood of color in her face, and the fact that she wouldn't look at him, he knew she had not wanted him to know about her night. Maybe he shouldn't have said anything, but it killed him to think that she would be afraid he'd be unkind to her about such a thing. And he needed her to know, for whatever lay in the future, that he was all in on the marriage. The good parts and the messy ones.

"Sadie." Her name came rough, and when her shoulders moved in a silent cry, Connor could no long fight the need to hold her. He moved from the chair to her bed and pulled her stiff frame into his arms.

"I asked Crystal not to tell you."

"I'm your husband."

She held herself rigid, swiping at the rolling tears, as if they irritated her. "We don't have that kind of marriage."

"Why can't we, Sadie?" He shifted so that he could see her, bracing a hand against the bed on the other side of her hip, then tipped her face so that she would see him. "Just because we didn't start off with some kind of storied romance? I don't think that's a good reason not to have a solid marriage."

Sniffing, she studied him, and the frustration in her expression drained away. "What does a solid marriage look like to you?"

Such a big question. Connor really pondered it, wondering if he could put words to all he felt and wanted for them. *Unashamed* drifted through his mind, and he wondered if, given their complicated past—and the lack of that storied romance he'd just mentioned in their present—if that was truly possible. "I want you to trust me, to believe that I won't malign your dignity, no matter how sick you get or what that illness does to you. I won't, Sadie. I swear to you, you never need to feel humiliated in front of me."

"But it *is* humiliating." A fresh tear slipped down her cheek, but she didn't swipe at it.

"I get that." He tugged on her shoulder, and she leaned toward him willingly. "I can definitely understand that." As he wrapped her snug against himself, he pressed another kiss against her head. "But just know, you're my wife—to me, that is sacred. An honor. I will never see you as less."

She didn't respond, but she stayed tucked against him. Connor wondered if she was trying to believe him or if she was simply retreating into silence.

Chapter Eighteen

(in which Reid plays at the neighbor's)

Two weeks after surgery they had a treatment plan in place—an aggressive blend of radiation and chemo.

Sadie experienced a mix of anxiety and relief at that. The next twelve weeks loomed before her like a terrifying mountain peak, but her doctor had breathed a fresh breath of hope of recovery. Added to that dichotomy, she rode a roller coaster of emotions concerning Connor.

He was so good with Reid, and watching them together melted Sadie's heart. It also gave her a yearning for things she knew she had no right to want as he worked his way into the soft places of her heart. Sharing their everyday lives also yielded a closeness that tempted her to forget that she'd put this situation on him, and he'd done it because he felt a divine compulsion to do so. She admired the good man Connor was. Longed for the affection he extended to be rooted in another place in his heart besides duty. And conversely—and sometimes frustratingly—resented that his care reminded her of her unworthiness and her neediness.

But all that Sadie buried deep within herself to wrestle with on her own. She certainly didn't need to complicate an already complicated situation with any of it.

When she felt well enough, she set herself purposefully toward making this arrangement as comfortable for Connor as she could. Daily, he got up early and ran, then worked long, stressful hours at the base tower. Added to the everyday wear of his job, he was also grappling with what to do when his contract with the air force expired. Though she could see in his eyes that he was tired when he came home in the evenings, he always took the time after he changed from BDUs to gym clothes to stretch out on the floor and play with Reid. At bedtime, he hauled Reid onto his lap and read to him.

His obvious efforts for her and her son inspired her. When their moms had been in town for her surgery, they'd stocked the small freezer in the apartment with ready-for-the-oven meals. Sadie made sure one of them was hot and ready to eat shortly after Connor got home. She kept the laundry caught up, making sure his work clothes were wrinkle-free and met the high standards of military dress. And in between spending time with Reid in his creative worlds of Legos, army guys, and Hot Wheels, Sadie worked on letters, numbers, and small words with her son.

Along the way she found nuggets of goodness to be grateful for. That big chunk of time spent with Reid—time she hadn't had before in her life as a single mom. Easy, delicious food that her mom and Connor's mom had left for them. A comfortable home—well, mostly comfortable—located close to the treatment center.

And Connor.

Thank You, Lord, for Connor. Even if ours isn't a marriage of love, he's good to us.

Her focus on gratitude sharpened after treatments began, because it became a lifeline. The combination of radiation therapy and chemo hit her hard, and she spent the days after treatments riding the hard waters of nausea, sinking under exhaustion, and dealing with the pains that came with the toxic but necessary therapies.

She ate little—she wasn't hungry, nothing tasted good, and often food stung the sores that developed in her mouth. Three weeks into her first cycle, Sadie wondered how she would make it through the remaining nine weeks of treatment. Not only that, but Connor still had a few weeks left with the air force. She hated her selfishness, but the days without him at home became long, and Reid was struggling with having only his sick mom for company.

Maybe she and Reid should have stayed in Sugar Pine with her parents after all.

The thought pricked stinging tears in her eyes as she rolled into a lying position on the couch one early afternoon. Sadie wasn't sure why—likely that was simply the exhaustion causing her emotions to be on hypermobility. But, well, this marrying Connor deal was supposed to make this easier. Wasn't it? At the moment, imagining being at her parents' house, with her mom and her dad there to keep Reid occupied so she didn't have to fight sleep, life didn't feel easier.

Squeezing her eyes shut, Sadie worked to settle the whirlwind of thoughts. Gratitude. That was what she needed to turn to. Forcing her hand toward the notebook and pen she'd laid on the coffee table in front of the couch, she took it up and found a clean page on which to write.

1. *Next week is a recovery week—no chemo or radiation.*

She held the promise of a break close to her heart in deep relief.

2. *Reid is starting to sound out simple words. Cat. Run. Sit.*

He was getting it, and she got to see his progress firsthand. That was a blessing.

3. *I don't have to drive down the mountain on a two-hour trek three days in a row for treatment, only to turn around and go back the same way after infusions are done.*

That was a really good thing.

4. *Mom and Dad are spared seeing me like this every day.*

She was thankful for that.

5. *Connor is*

Thoughts jumbled, Sadie held her pen midmotion above the page. Connor was kind. He took good care of them. And sometimes, she caught him staring at her like...

Like he felt sorry for her. She didn't write any of that.

As a bitter ache stirred, her list-making practice was cut short by a knock at the door. Setting aside her notebook, she placed her feet on the floor and summoned the energy to move.

"Mommy, who's that?" Reid looked at her from his spot on the floor, his hands paused in midair with two jets that Connor had bought him last week.

"I don't know, buddy." Sadie pushed herself upright, waited for the world to stop rocking and rolling, and then stepped toward the entry. "I'll go see, okay?"

"Maybe it's my new friend!"

Connor's neighbors downstairs had a boy Reid's age, Liam. *Add that to the list—Reid has a friend.* She'd met them—the mother's name was Mandi—a couple of days before she'd started treatments. Connor had taken Reid out to the park a few times with Hansen, the dad, and Liam. Reid had a blast every outing.

"Maybe." Sadie shuffled to the door. She wasn't up for company, so she selfishly hoped whoever was on the other side had a package that they'd leave and then disappear.

Not to be.

"It is!" Reid bounced his way to the doorway as soon as Sadie had it opened. "Hi, Liam! I was hoping it was you!"

For Reid's sake—he was so enthusiastic, and she couldn't blame him—and for Mandi's, who stood with a smile pointed at her from the hallway, Sadie roused what she hoped looked like excitement. "How about that, buddy. You guessed it."

Mandi put a staying hand on Liam just before her black-haired son raced into the apartment. "Hi, Sadie, how are you feeling?"

"I'm okay." Sadie wasn't sure if that was a lie. *No, I am okay. We're still in one piece, right? Add that to the list too.*

Empathy scrawled on Mandi's face as she tipped her head. "You look like you could use a nice long nap." A tender smile smoothed the woman's expression. "That's why we're here. I wondered if I could take Reid down to our place for the rest of the day? The boys have so much fun together—it'll be no trouble at all, I'm sure. I'll bring him back late this afternoon, and some supper for you guys as well."

A sudden urge to bawl overtook Sadie as she blinked. "Seriously?" Nearly the moment she'd decided that this move hadn't been a good idea, here was a gracious reprieve. Almost as if sent.

Would You do that, Lord? For me?

"Yeah." Mandi said. "I wanted to offer one day last week, but I had a sore throat, and I didn't want to risk exposing you to it. But I'm shipshape, and we would love to have Reid, if you're okay with it?"

One glance at Sadie's son was all she needed. He was all jumping beans and excited grins. His joy pulled a soft chuckle from her, and the kind gesture wrapped Sadie's heart with warmth. "That would be wonderful. Reid has been bored out of his mind—I haven't been a very fun companion for him lately."

"You need to rest." Mandi nodded firmly. "And like I said, the boys have so much fun together. One of these days, when you're better, we'll have to grab coffee or something and take them to a park. I'd love to get to know you better."

"I'd like that." A bit flustered, Sadie touched Reid's head and then knelt in front of him. "Will you be a good boy?"

"Yes, ma'am."

Sadie grinned at that response—courtesy of Connor, the military dad. Not a bad thing at all. "Good." She stood again. "I can come down and get him, if you'd rather?"

"Not at all. You just rest. I'll bring him, along with a casserole, up around four or five. Will that work?"

"Sure."

"And you have my number, right?"

"Yes. Connor wrote it on a sticky note and put it on the fridge."

"Perfect. We're set then." Mandi smiled at Reid. "Ready?"

"Yeah!" hollered both boys at the same time.

After Sadie waved and then shut the door, she listened to the excited duet as they made great plans for a Nerf battle.

"Thank You, Lord, for these little gifts. Thank You for seeing me." Tipping her head against the door, she whispered her grateful prayer.

As she shuffled back to the couch, grabbing a thick afghan as she went, she thought to finish writing out her thankful list. A good idea, but one that remained only in her mind. As soon as she lay down, the weight and warmth of the afghan overpowered her intent. She slept deeply, with gratitude and a sense of being held.

***

A text alert came through on Connor's phone before he started his car to go home for the day.

Reid is at our place still. When I went up to your apartment, Sadie was still out. I didn't want to wake her, so I left the casserole in the oven and brought Reid back down with us. Hope that's okay!

Connor inhaled sharply as Mandi's acts of kindness made his chest squeeze. *Thanks*, he texted back. *I'll get him on my way up. Be there in five.*

After receiving Mandi's thumbs-up response, Connor turned the engine on and headed home. His thoughts quickly shifted to Sadie, and they changed to prayer almost immediately. *Please, Father, lend her Your strength.* Nearly finished with her first cycle, his wife was struggling, and it hurt to watch her suffer like this. While that pain made its way through his chest, Connor also found something to be thankful for in it. He was glad to be with her, glad she wasn't in this alone. He wondered if Sadie knew how much he wanted to help her. Sometimes he had the impression that she thought he might feel resentful, that this obligation he'd taken on was only that: an obligation.

Maybe that was where this thing started, but it wasn't how he felt. He loved that he had a family to come home to every night. His life felt fuller and more purposeful. Having Reid to play with, while maybe counterintuitive, gave him an outlet of joy every night. And seeing Sadie every day...

He didn't know what the words were for that, other than not even two months into this marriage and he didn't want to go back to life without her and Reid. What had been lonely—though he hadn't felt lonely at the time—was now full. What had been incomplete—without his awareness—now felt whole.

This was the life he was meant for. Connor knew it to the marrow of his bones. If only he could make that clear to his wife.

Having reached the apartments, Connor parked and then strode toward Hansen and Mandi's ground-level place. Reid flung himself at Connor's legs the moment he passed through the door.

"Daddy! Guess what? Me and Liam played all day!"

Lifting his little guy, he hugged him. "That's awesome. What do you say to Mrs. Hunt?"

"Thank you." Reid tucked against Connor's shoulder, suddenly shy.

"Anytime," Mandi said, ruffling his hair. "Thanks for being so good."

"Was he?" Connor asked.

"Absolutely."

"Good job, son." Connor hugged Reid closer and then nodded to Mandi. "Thanks again. Sadie needed a day to rest."

"Glad to help. We'll find a day next week to do it again."

Connor and Reid headed to their own place, Reid riding in Connor's arms. Once in their apartment, Connor glanced to the couch.

Snuggled in the afghan his grandmother had crocheted for his high school graduation gift, Sadie still slept. The sight of her, peaceful and lovely, made his heart trip. Even ill, his wife was a beautiful woman. He set Reid on the carpet in the living room and moved to check on her. Her skin was warm to the touch—possibly she was running a fever, but it wasn't too high. She sighed and shifted, and Connor backed away. As he did, the open notebook on the table caught his attention. A list...

He wasn't sure what the list was exactly, but at the end of it he caught his name. Number five, two simple words: *And Connor.* Nothing else. He looked back at Sadie, curiosity tumbling in his mind. What had she meant by it? Was that her complete thought, or had she been interrupted?

Reid slipped his hand into Connor's. "Daddy, Mommy's still sleeping."

"Yeah, buddy," Connor whispered. "Let's be quiet so she can rest, okay?"

"Yes, sir." Reid held a salute.

Connor lifted him again and carried Reid to the master bedroom, plopping him onto the king-sized bed. "What did you do at Liam's today?"

Reid chattered happily about his afternoon at Liam's while Connor changed. There was a Nerf battle, kites, a snack of grapes and cheese and crackers. When Connor was stripped down to only his pants, Reid suddenly burst into giggles.

"You have furry armpits!"

Startled for only a moment, Connor suppressed a laugh. Raising an arm, he examined the hair there like this was news. "Look at that. I sure do. Do you?"

Reid pulled on his shirt and lifted his arm to check. "Nope."

"Let me see." Connor held the skinny arm up and poked at Reid's side. A smattering of laughter erupted from his little body, and Reid squirmed as Connor tickled.

"Sounds like too much fun in here." Sadie's voice had Connor whipping his attention from Reid to the door. She leaned against the frame, arms crossed. Though weariness lingered in her eyes, she smiled.

And Connor... The two words punched back into his mind as he met Sadie's stare. Possibly it was sleep, but he swore there was a softness there that he hadn't seen from her before. He wanted to know what she thought. How she felt. Letting his gaze drift over her face, he took in her loveliness. Her smooth skin, a little pink with warmth. The curve of her jaw, the lines of which he yearned to trace with his fingertips. The arch of her brows. The shape of her mouth...

Suddenly he was very aware of the throb of his pulse.

Reid wiggled off the bed and ran to his mother. "Mommy, did you sleep all day?"

Slowly moving her attention from Connor to Reid—as if she wasn't sure she wanted to—Sadie nodded. "I must have."

"We came up before Daddy came home, but you were still sleeping. So Miss Mandi put food in the oven and said to stay with her until Daddy's home."

"That was kind of her." Sadie looked back at Connor, uncertainty in her expression.

"It was." Connor pushed off the bed and stood. "And she wouldn't want you to feel bad. You needed to rest, and she was glad to help."

Sadie touched Reid's shoulder, insecurity written in her furrowed brow. "How about you go wash your hands for supper?"

Reid saluted and skipped down the hall. Sadie pushed off the doorframe but didn't turn to go like Connor thought she would. Instead, he felt her gaze on him as he walked toward the dresser to grab a T-shirt. A spark jolted through his veins at the sensation that there was appreciation in her study. Battling the sensation that was quickly turning his thoughts toward things of a more intimate nature, Connor ducked into his shirt and turned to ask her how she was feeling.

The look she held on him was his undoing.

In five slow strides, he stood in front of her. She lifted her chin to hold the connection between them. Connor raised his hand and tenderly brushed the curve of her jaw. Her unwavering gaze was gravity—an irresistible force that pulled him nearer. When his lips brushed hers, he found them soft and warm. He moved his hand to cup her neck. For several breathless, euphoric moments he tested the willingness of her mouth, aware of the throb of her pulse against his palm and the gentle hold of her hand on his arm. Her soft response against his mouth was inviting and irresistible.

When he slid his other hand over her waist to her back, stepping so close that his thighs brushed hers, Sadie ducked away. The break of her kiss hit him with a cold blast. Her scurried retreat swiftly dashed away the exhilaration of mingled breath and shared longing, replacing it with harsh disappointment.

"Sadie," he whispered.

She refused to look at him, turning toward the hallway instead. "I'll get supper on the table."

Connor watched her retreat and then turned to lean backward against the doorframe. Shutting his eyes, he rolled his fists as an instant, visceral replay scrawled through his mind. The way she'd looked at him, the firm hold she laid on his arm, and the way she'd kissed him back. It had a been a moment with everything going in the right direction. One of promising hope for things to turn out the way his heart had become set upon. More than a small hint that she wanted the same.

What had gone wrong?

Chapter Nineteen

(in which new plans are made)

Connor answered Jackson's phone call on the third ring. "Hi, brother." Having just finished his morning jog, he lowered onto a picnic table bench in the budding shade of a tree near the creek.

"How are things?" Jackson asked.

Connor didn't need to ask for clarification on what things. Jackson texted him now and then, as did Matt.

"Things are okay, sort of." He leaned back and drew in a cool breath of spring air. Sadie had still been in bed when he'd left, which was normal, as he went out early. That morning he'd sat on the mattress beside her before he'd walked out of the room, daring to finger the hair that had drifted over her pretty face while she slept. Silently, he prayed over her—for her day, for her time with Reid, and for her recovery. Sadie hadn't moved, and though the temptation was strong, he didn't risk disrupting her sleep by kissing her brow before he rose to leave.

But he'd thought about it. Truth be known, he'd thought of it on many occasions. More so now after the kiss they'd shared a few days before. The kiss that had knotted tension between them, as well as pinning his heart with a strong and clear longing to hold his wife, to move past this sense of being in a marriage of obligation and into one of mutual joy and contentment. It'd been what he'd wanted all along—something that looked like his parents' relationship, rather than the stilted, awkward one he and Sadie were currently limping along in.

Connor wasn't willing to share all that with Jackson.

Maintaining privacy felt necessary.

"Sort of?" Jackson pressed.

Connor sat forward, mind made up. His heart felt too raw to go into it at the moment. "Sadie's recovering from her first round of treatments. It's been rough, and the doctors warn that the next two will probably be harder."

"How are you two though?"

"You're nosy."

"Just trying to be there for you, Connor. You were for me."

There was that.

"We're still trying to figure out how this marriage will work."

"I hope that's not as ominous as it sounds."

"There's no danger of a split, if that's what you mean."

"Good. But no, that's not all that I meant. Are you okay?"

Connor had to admit, even if Jackson's pushiness was a touch annoying, it was nice to know his brother cared. "Yeah, I'm okay. Let's just say that you were right. It's harder than I thought."

"I read that loud and clear." Jackson held a silent beat, likely deciding if he was going to push for more from Connor. He changed topics instead. "Are you guys going to go to Mom and Dad's in a couple of weeks? Mom says she's got plans."

"I heard about that." Mom had called him yesterday with the invitation. He wasn't sure what she was up to, but he suspected there would be a baby shower for Matt and Lauren.

"She says Jacob and Kate are coming this time." A tinge of bitterness edged Jackson's voice. "We'll see if that actually happens."

Connor's thoughts moved warily to Jacob, and a heaviness settled in his chest. A phone call from days before had lodged it there. "Go easy on Jacob, Jackson."

"What?"

"Just go easy on him." Jacob was in trouble—he didn't share the whole story, Connor was sure, but there was no disguising the defeat in Jacob's voice that day. Didn't matter that Jackson and Jacob had conflicting personalities and an ongoing life battle. Right now, Jacob needed his family's support. More than ever.

"Why should I?"

Connor didn't wish to betray Jacob's trust, so he wouldn't divulge what had been entrusted to him. But there were other good reasons for Jackson to back off. "Because you don't know what it was like for him to grow up as the one who didn't need much."

"What does that mean?"

A memory, over fifteen years old, pressed into Connor's mind. He'd found Jacob out in the woods alone, a pillow lashed to a tree trunk with a belt, and Jacob's fists bright red and swelling because that pillow absorbed only some of the blows. Along with pummeling a pillow strapped to a tree, his brother had been crying. It took some time to get the story out, but it boiled down to a pretty big hurt. Jacob had earned an award for being the top student in his grade, and there'd been a brunch for it. Mom had forgotten about it. She'd been wrapped up with phone calls about something related to Jackson's medical needs.

Even there, under the spring trees as a full-grown man, Connor felt the sadness of seeing Jacob's pain. Mom hadn't meant for it to happen, and in front of the family, Jacob had brushed it off as not a big deal. But it had been a very big deal—and the reality was that situation hadn't been an isolated occurrence.

Connor weighed telling Jackson about that time, but he'd promised Jacob he wouldn't tell anyone. The loyalty branded into Connor's soul wouldn't allow a betrayal, even now so many years later. But that didn't mean Connor couldn't speak up in general terms.

"It means that Jacob was self-reliant and bold almost since birth," Connor said. "Which often meant that everyone figured he was good on his own. Managed to be a good student without much help. Stayed out of trouble. Was ambitious. All of that allowed Mom and Dad to focus their attention elsewhere. Matt, when he would get into trouble. Me, when I struggled in school. You, with all of the medical needs that came with your cleft lip. Then later, with the younger boys. You're a middle kid, Jackson, so I would think you'd understand what it's like to get lost in the shuffle of things."

"Okay, I can get that. But we're grown men. What does this have to do with anything now?"

"Not much, except you really don't know him well, and all you've got for him is resentment."

"How did this conversation turn on me?" Offense rang loud and clear in Jackson's voice. "I called to check up on you, brother. Out of the goodness of my heart."

"Yeah, and thanks for that." Connor wished he didn't feel the prodding to interfere. He really didn't like his brothers being upset with him on any occasions—preferred easy relationships. Who didn't? But sometimes, some things just needed to be addressed, and for some reason, he was the brother commissioned to say hard things. "Seriously, I appreciate it. And I'm not saying everything is all on you when it comes to you and Jacob. It's just that living with this tension between Sadie and me made me think of how exhausting it must be for you and for Jacob. Do you really want that to be how things are forever?"

"I haven't wanted it to be the way things are now."

"Okay, so all I'm saying is, go easy on him. Or better yet, make an effort to build a bridge."

"That's going to be one long bridge." Jackson let the sarcastic comment die almost before he finished it and then sighed. "Okay. I'll make a better effort when we're together. You're coming though, right?"

"Yeah, I think so. Want to see that niece of mine again before she starts walking. But I need to talk to Sadie first—she'll be finishing up her second cycle by then and probably won't feel great. We'll likely stay at her parents' if we go."

"Understandable. Think Tyler will be there?"

Man, there was that too. His parents hadn't shared a lot of details, but Connor knew enough to know that Tyler was in trouble, and the long haul didn't look promising. Why, all of the sudden, did it seem like the Murphy family was stepping into darkness? "Dad hasn't said much, other than to pray hard for him. I doubt Tyler will be out that soon though."

"That's what I thought too."

A pause drifted over the call. In it, Connor felt the weight of everything, and it made breathing hard. How could he help his brothers when his life in his own home wasn't settled?

"Connor?"

"Yeah."

"You don't always have to take care of everyone. You do know that, right?"

Connor hummed an ambiguous answer.

"Seriously. Sometimes it's okay for you to admit you need something from someone else too."

Standing up to stretch, Connor thought about that, even after he and Jackson's conversation ended. He wondered how that would turn out, if he told Sadie he needed something from her. Considering that it was her whole heart he wanted, he wasn't sure that gamble was safe.

Then again, if he was gleaning anything from his brothers, it was that some things simply needed to be addressed.

***

Days after the kiss, conversation still felt stiff and chilled. Seeing that she was upset at him, Connor shelved that quiet impulse to take the risk and tell her how he really felt. Instead, after he read a short bedtime story to Reid and Sadie tucked him in, Connor brought up the proposed trip to Sugar Pine.

"My mom is organizing something," he started as he lowered onto the opposite side of the couch where Sadie sat. Wrapped in her long oatmeal-colored sweater with a steaming mug of tea in her hands, she looked like she could use a good cuddling. He'd gladly volunteer, but he wasn't up for creating more tension between them.

"Is she? What's she got going?"

"My guess is a baby shower for Matt and Lauren, but I'm not sure. She called and asked if we'd be willing to go up there for a weekend."

"When?"

"Two weeks."

Sadie sipped her drink, her expression thoughtful. "You'll be officially done with the air force then."

"That's true." He pulled in a deep breath. The future still looked hazy. All he knew at the moment was that they needed to stay where they were until Sadie's treatments were complete. He had some funds set aside—enough for three months' worth of living expenses. But after that... He and Sadie would need to talk. Hopefully by then, these hard walls between them wouldn't feel so insurmountable. "You'll be just finished with your second cycle though. I know you're not going to feel like visiting."

Her eyes lifted to his for a moment, and in that brief contact, he felt a softening from her. She nodded. "Probably not. But if we could stay at my parents, it might be nice. Reid would enjoy it."

Discomfort wound in him as he asked the next question. "When you say we, do you mean me too?"

Shifting as if she wanted to hide, Sadie rearranged her sweater and took another drink. "Unless you'd rather stay with your family."

"You are my family."

"You know what I meant."

Connor ran his hands along his thighs, wondering if he should chase the underlying problem with that little exchange. He decided he wasn't up for it. "I'd rather stay where you and Reid stay. I assumed that would be your parents' place."

"Okay then." Her voice sounded almost mouse-ish, as if the idea of him being with her in her parents' home was mortifying.

A response that was really defeating.

"Okay." He stared at the table in front of the couch, trying to keep his heart from plunging into despair.

Chapter Twenty

(in which Connor and Sadie finally discuss the kiss)

It was only a small kiss. Connor is, after all, just a man.

During her years of rebellion and recklessness, Sadie had discovered that most men were impulsive and physical. A kiss didn't carry the same meaning to them as it did to her. For a long time, she'd tried to convince herself that she could be as casual with such intimacies as the men she'd given them to. Too late, she'd discovered that could never be true of her.

Kisses weren't meaningless to her.

As she tried to reason with herself over her morning tea several days after said event, Sadie stared at the grain of the table beneath her propped-up elbows. Connor wasn't like the majority of men she'd encountered in those wayward years. Actually, he wasn't like most men at all. He lived and breathed honor. Would he consider what happened in the doorway of their shared bedroom a meaningless kiss?

She could just ask him instead of agonizing over it. That would be the grown-up thing to do. Perhaps if she did, this fresh grip of anxiety she felt whenever they were together would loosen. She would feel like she could meet his gaze and not feel...heartbroken?

That might be extreme.

No, it wasn't. She felt heartbroken when she was near him. Or thought of him.

Which was perhaps why she felt like she couldn't ask. If he said it had meant nothing to him—just a moment of...something superficial—then her disappointment might plunge into something worse. Sadie wasn't sure she should do that to either of them.

The quietness of the apartment rustled away as the sound of Connor and Reid coming back neared the front door. Being Saturday, Connor had taken Reid out to the park and then to grab breakfast.

"Mommy! Liam came too, and guess what?" Reid was sharing his exciting news with her before he was even fully in the apartment. "Daddy says that we can go see Pops and Nana in two weeks!" He stopped halfway between her and the door, Connor behind him, and looked up at the man. "How long is two weeks?"

"Fourteen days." Connor stepped around Reid and continued toward the table, where Sadie sat. After he set a cup of something in front of her as well as a take-out bag from the bagel place on base, he paused. Tentatively he bent until he pressed a cautious kiss to her hair.

Maybe she should ask him. She could be brave, couldn't she?

"Fourteen days!" Reid flopped himself around like one of those windsock guys at a car lot. "That's too long. I thought two weeks was going to be short."

Sadie peeked up at Connor, wondering if her son's childishness was going to earn a stern rebuke.

Connor leaned against the table and crossed his arms. "It'll go by faster than you think, buddy."

Relief eased through her, though she chided herself for being worried. Connor wasn't unreasonable in his expectations.

Reid held up his hands. "I don't even have that many fingers!"

A low chuckle came from the man near her, the sound of it making Sadie grin.

"No, you sure don't." Connor pushed back to standing and walked toward Reid to swoop him up. "How about we make a counting chain? You can take one link off every day until it's time to go."

"A counting chain?"

"Yep. My mom—your Grams—used to make them with us boys before Christmas."

"What do you make them with?"

"Strips of paper." Connor plopped Reid onto the couch and playfully poked his belly. "We'll go to the store in a bit to get some colorful construction paper and glue, okay? It'll be our project for the afternoon."

Sadie guessed Reid nodded, but she wasn't sure.

"Right now I need to talk to your mom." Connor glanced at Sadie. "Find something to play with for a while, okay, Airman?"

Her next guess was that her son saluted. Again, she couldn't see him to be sure, but Connor held a salute, so it seemed likely. Reid then scurried off the couch and down the hall to his room.

At Connor's approach, Sadie's stomach began to do a twisting thing that somehow made her blush. He scooted a chair closer to her and lowered onto it.

Sadie traced the letters on the paper cup Connor had brought her. "A counting chain is a good idea."

"Thanks."

Quiet settled between them. The tight, achy kind that made every second feel like ten and every breath strained. Connor reached out, his touch featherlight as he grazed the back of her hand and then pulled away.

"Are you mad at me?" he asked softly.

Raising her chin, she looked at him in surprise. "Mad at you? Why would I be?"

"I don't know, but the past several days have been..." He pushed forked fingers through his cropped hair, his jaw tight as he searched for what he wanted to say. Then he looked at her again, the space between his brow lined. "Maybe I shouldn't have kissed you. I thought you were upset that I did."

He'd felt the tension too, then. As heat washed her face, Sadie looked back at the cup Connor had set in front of her.

"Are you?" he pressed.

"No." She blinked, working up the courage to ask what she

wanted to know. "Maybe."

Connor sat back, his shoulders slumped. "Then I'm sorry that I did it."

"Did you mean it?"

"What?"

Sadie took a deep breath. "Why did you kiss me?"

As he stared at her, clearly not sure what to say, she could see the pulse in his neck leap. "Because I wanted to."

"But...I mean what I..." Sadie stopped fumbling over her words and closed her lips. This was not going very adult-like at all. In fact, she felt like a twelve-year-old. "Can I ask you something that is none of my business?"

He flinched at that. "You can ask me anything, Sadie. It's all your business."

He thought that? She swallowed, drew a breath, and plunged in. "How many girls have you kissed?"

"Two." His lack of hesitation shocked her.

"Two?" That answer shocked her even more. "Two, besides me?"

"No. Two including you."

"Oh." Not what she was expecting, and a blast of shame blindsided her. She'd have to think pretty hard to remember how many men she'd kissed. "That's...unusual."

"Unusual, bad?" Now he sounded insecure.

"No." She fidgeted with the cup and then pulled her hands into her lap. He'd only kissed her and Ivy? He hadn't kissed another woman since? Connor was twenty-seven years old—how was that even possible?

He shifted beside her, and suddenly his hands were around hers. "Now my turn."

A sour heat plunged through her gut. Surely he knew how she'd lived before returning to Sugar Pine. Would he really make her confess everything to him, when he already knew how ashamed she was of her life?

"Why were you mad at me for kissing you?"

Oh. Relief washed away the ugliness, but tears still pricked her eyes. She tried to blink them away. "Because I thought you didn't mean it."

One hand lifted, and with the tips of his fingers on her chin, he coaxed her to look at him again. "Why?"

"Because I pushed you into this. Marrying me wasn't your idea, and now your life is so much more complicated."

"I distinctly remember proposing to you."

"After I asked you first."

"You didn't ask me—not seriously. Do you really think I would do something like this if I didn't want to?"

"Yes."

"What?"

"You're completely honor and duty bound. On top of that, you think that my life, my mistakes, are partly your fault. Why else would you bring flowers to my parents every year? Why would you keep praying for me all this time?"

"Because I care about you and about your parents."

"But not...not the way that kiss implied. That was just..."

"Just what?"

The silence thickened as Sadie tried to find an answer. She couldn't. But neither was she willing to allow her heart to believe what he was implying. "Did you ever consider, in all these years, that maybe *I* was the one who ruined *your* life?"

Connor stared at her dumbfounded. "How do you figure that?"

"I keep thinking—especially after that kiss—that if I hadn't been so selfish and so obsessed with you back in high school, that I would have turned you down for the dance. You and Ivy could have talked things out, and you might be with her today if I hadn't been in the middle of it." Sadie's vision swam as she let what she truly feared tumble out into the open between them. "You wouldn't be stuck with a sick woman who will only leave you with more regret and heartache—not to mention a boy who isn't really your son."

At that, anger darkened his eyes. "Don't do that. Don't say that. I love Reid, and I couldn't love him more even if his DNA matched mine. I don't regret him, and I won't ever. I *want* to be his dad."

Connor gripped both of her hands and pulled them to his chest. "And you—I have no thought of Ivy or anything about our past when I'm with you. This isn't about guilt. I kissed you because I'm falling in love with my wife. She's this beautiful, tender woman who fills my heart a little more every day. Sadie, I think about you all the time, and when I'm with you, I want to hold your hand. I want to take care of you and make you happy. And more and more often, I want to kiss that pretty mouth until we're both breathless."

Sadie blinked as her tears streamed, her heart at once fearful to take in what he was saying and yet desperate to plunge into it. "Connor, I'm not sure you should fall in love with me."

"Why?" Desperation pulled in his voice.

She shook her head, mixed up in big emotions about the past, the present, and the future.

"Because you think that if you don't get better, it'll hurt me more, don't you?" Connor wrapped both arms around her, then slid her from her chair to his lap. "Losing you, if that's what happens, will hurt, Sadie. There's no avoiding that—and just so we're clear, I'm really praying that God will heal you and we'll have a long lifetime together, full of breathless kisses. But either way, we have a choice how we live today. What if we leave everything behind us in the past? Wouldn't that open the possibility that the life we have now—this gift that is you and me together, for however long this life may last—could be beautiful?"

Leaning her head against his shoulder, Sadie shut her eyes. The storm in her heart and mind settled, but a sense of unworthiness lingered. Even without the mistakes of their past, all she was was a sick woman in need of help. She had no job, no particular skills. Now, thanks to cancer, she couldn't even give him more children. She was a leech on him, a parasite living on his goodness. "I have nothing to offer you, Connor."

He tucked his head against hers. "What about your love?"

"It doesn't seem like enough."

With hands on either side of her head, he held her face and pressed his forehead to hers. "But it's what I want most." Emotion made his voice wobble, and then he nuzzled her cheek and neck.

Sadie gave into the warm floating sensation as he kissed her exposed skin near the collar of her shirt. His breath warmed her neck as he slowly moved to kiss the place beneath her ear, and she had to grip his shirt to keep from swooning straight to the floor. When his mouth touched hers, she sighed into him. The saltiness of tears—hers as well as his—mingled in their kisses.

"Please love me, Sadie," he murmured against her, breathless.

She wrapped her arms around him, and he held her in return.

"I do," she said. "I do love you, Connor Murphy."

As he kissed her again, Sadie's thoughts flashed to that thankful list in her notebook—to that unfinished entry. *And Connor...* She'd meant to write that he was good to Reid, and yes, she was thankful for that. But actually, she was just thankful for him.

Mentally, she amended her entry to read, *Connor, the man who loves me.*

The one whom she loved.

Chapter Twenty-One

(in which there is hope for the future)

"You'll be okay?" Standing on his parents' back deck, Connor stood behind his wife, hands running the length of her arms until he twined his fingers with hers and then wrapped her tight against him.

She leaned back with a contented sigh, a sound like music to his heart. "I'll be good. I feel stronger this round, which doesn't make sense."

Sadie had seemed stronger that round. She was more settled, happier. Perhaps because the doctors were a little more positive about a good outcome than they had been initially. Or maybe it had nothing to do with doctors at all. Maybe it had to do with long evenings spent snuggled up together on the couch. Or nights spent tangled in each other's arms. And surely lingering, breathless kisses didn't hurt.

A thrill spiraled through him at those memories, and Connor dipped his mouth to the soft curve of her neck. He contented himself with a small taste of her sun-warmed skin, knowing that she'd willingly return his attentions later.

Stepping back, he turned her to face him and adjusted her sweater to protect her from the chilly spring breeze. "Mom will keep your mug full of cider."

"I have no doubt."

"We'll just be on the trail to the ridge." He pointed across the backyard. "Not far out at all."

Sadie laughed. "I'll be fine, Connor. Reid is enamored with

Bobbie Joy, your mom is enamored with both, and your sisters-in-law are staying too. Go hang out with your brothers. We'll be just fine."

Connor stared into her happy blue eyes. *Happy.* Man, he had longed to see that looking back up at him. He fought a temptation to push his fingers into her hair, knowing he might pull out a few strands or even a clump. Sadie had cried when the first fistful had come free the week before. But since, she'd come to accept it. Tomorrow, she had an appointment in town to cut it all off.

Sorrow touched his heart as he thought about that. Sadie's hair was beautiful.

Sadie is beautiful. More, he loved her. Whatever haircut she ended up with wasn't going to change that.

Connor bent to kiss her. "I love you, Sadie Murphy."

"Love you too." Sadie smiled against his lips and then pushed him back. "Now get out of here. Don't come back until you're good and dirty and you smell like a woodsman."

"You'd like that, huh?"

"Absolutely." She winked.

Chuckling, Connor turned to stride across the deck and clomp down the stairs.

Jackson met him at the bottom, nudging him with an elbow. "Things are getting better, eh?"

With a grin, Connor stiff-armed him.

Not to be put off, Jackson scrambled right back in step with him. "Come on—tell me."

"Things are better," Connor said.

"Great." The mischievous sound of Jackson's response put Connor on high alert. With this particular brother, anything could happen.

"What are you up to?"

"Why would you assume I'm up to something?"

Connor eyed him.

"Hey." Jackson held his hands up. "I'm not the one who organized an all-out attack on a certain newlywed couple on their first morning at Mom and Dad's."

The memory of the full-scale Nerf and Silly String attack on Jackson and Mackenzie eighteen months before made Connor laugh out loud. "No, but you wish you had come up with it."

"What? Kenz was mortified."

"No way. That was the reason she stayed with you." Not even close to true, and the real story behind that miracle was a lot more messy and a whole lot less funny than that moment. But still, it'd been funny. And Jackson, the prankster, totally deserved it.

"What are you boys bickering about?" Matt met the pair as they neared the trail at the back of the long yard.

"Whether or not it had been a good idea to initiate Kenz into the Murphy clan that first day she was here."

Matt nodded. "It was brilliant, if I do say so myself."

"Come on, man." Connor shot Matt a look. "Don't go pretending you came up with it. That was me."

"No way."

"The logistics. The execution." Connor crossed his arms and set a military stance. "That was *all* me."

"Are you guys gonna hike today, or are we just gonna stand here and discuss whose dumb ideas are better?" Jacob stalked from behind and passed through the group without stopping.

Jackson eyed Jacob's back as he walked into the thick of the woods. "You know who has it coming?"

"Take it easy, Jack," Connor said.

"I'm not being mean." Jackson started after Jacob. "I'm just saying someone needs help unwinding his whitey-tighties."

Together, Matt and Connor walked behind the feuding men, exchanging a glance. "And you think you're a good one to do that?" Connor asked in a low voice.

Jackson flung a cavalier wave. "I'm always a good one for that." With that, he broke into a trot, clearly intending to catch up with Jacob.

This had *uncomfortable afternoon* written all over it. Why was Jackson being so bullheaded about this? How hard could it be to just leave Jacob alone?

Connor shot another glance at Matt.

"You thinking what I'm thinking?" Matt asked.

"That this is not going to end well?"

"Exactly." Matt rolled his shoulders back. "We'd best get up there." And then he was off, running up the trail after the other two.

So much for an easy hike and a relaxing day with his brothers. Good grief, he should have stayed with Sadie. She was a lot more fun than playing referee for his brothers was going to be. Be that as it may, Connor double timed it, the incline of the trail causing the back of his legs to burn.

The three ahead of him must have moved into a death sprint, because all of them vanished into the woods up ahead. After a deep pull of air, Connor pushed his pace.

At the snap of a twig to his right, he slowed. Likely, it was nothing. Wild things were usually small and harmless out here, especially in the daylight. But then there was a crash in the brush, followed by a hair-raising scream. The sound was unhuman and made Connor's blood run cold. Worse, it was followed by a low and distinctive growl.

Mountain lion.

Connor froze. Big cats were fast, and running would trigger their predatory instinct. Oh man, his brothers—

With a shout, Jacob suddenly burst from the area to Connor's right, a little bit above where Connor had stopped.

"Run!" Jacob shouted. Connor spied a sickening red oozing down his arm before Jacob bolted up the trail again.

"Jake! Stop running!"

His brother paid no heed. Another nerve-tingling growl sounded from the woods, and Connor lost his resolve to stay planted. He shot off after Jacob, heart pounding in his throat. Every ten steps or so, he glanced behind him, terrified a big cat would be nearly ready to maul him. Sooner than he ever had before, he reached the small clearing of the ridge, and seeing his brothers gathered there, heaving for air and watching him run their way, Connor grabbed the nearest decent-sized deadfall branch and took up a defensive stance between the lower trail and the clearing.

"Stay back! There's a cougar down there." With his back to his brothers, he scanned the woods below. "Jacob, are you okay?"

Silence. And then...

Roaring shouts of laughter.

Connor stood from his ready-fight position, lowering his makeshift weapon. Slowly he turned.

Matt. Jacob. Jackson. All three held their bellies while they nearly teared up with laughter. From his right, Brayden strolled from the cover of woods into the clearing, also busting a gut.

He held up his phone, the camera lens pointed at Connor. "Sadie will be glad to know she married such a warrior," Brayden snickered.

The chorus of laughter crescendoed, and Brandon made his appearance, emerging from the trail below, laughing and waving his phone in the air. From it came the growling mountain lion.

Setup. Connor had walked right into it. Jackson had practically warned him down in the backyard minutes before... But still Connor had taken the bait. He pivoted and pointed his finger at Jackson. "You!"

Jackson could barely stand he was laughing so hard, but he pointed at Jacob.

"You?" Unbelievable. Jacob? Granted, it was his "bloody" arm that had sold the whole setup. But still, Jacob executing a practical joke? No way. "There's not a chance you came up with this, Jacob. This reeks of Jackson."

Then again, the ketchup-turned-fake blood *was* running down Jacob's arm, not Jackson's. What the—

"You're right. I wouldn't come up with something like this." Jacob walked toward Connor and clapped his shoulder, still snickering. "But it sure was funny."

"Really?" Connor was having a hard time keeping his grin buttoned down. Who would have thought, Jackson and Jacob in cahoots? Miracles in the Murphy clan never ceased.

"For real, though, Connor, you were quite the hero." Matt

came forward too, in control of his laughter enough to talk. "Ready to take on the big cat for us all."

"That was a good one, Jackson." Brayden went for a fist bump. "Perfectly designed, as always."

"Yeah," Connor also extended a fist to Jackson and then to Jacob. "That was pretty good. Glad Sadie wasn't with us though."

Jackson smirked. "All part of the plan."

As the adrenaline settled, the brothers found a place to stretch out in the sun. Scattered over the area of the clearing, they each faced the eastern view that all of them had loved throughout their lives.

Brandon tossed a stick over the edge and then leaned back on his palms. "Wish Tyler was here."

A round of muffled *yeahs* came from the other boys, and a heaviness pushed away any remnants of laughter. Connor rubbed his chest and squeezed his eyes shut, thinking about how much Dad must be hurting these days. Tyler and Dad were close. Nearly business partners. Not having him there had to be painful, especially since Dad likely took more than his fair share of the blame for it all.

"Lauren's got this thing about memorizing Scripture," Matt said quietly. "She says that way she has it close by when life demands a God view. Anyway, she quotes this verse when things seems out of control. 'The LORD sits enthroned over the flood. The LORD is enthroned as king forever.' Maybe we can remember that as we pray for our brother."

Connor looked up at the leaves and scattering of pine branches over his head. *You are King over the flood. The chaos in our lives. You spoke to the winds and the waves, and they were still. You have brought a miracle of love and happiness into my life. Please, Lord, reign over Tyler too.*

Not another word was spoken about Tyler, but Connor was certain their brother wouldn't leave their hearts or minds. The silence eased, and small talk was exchanged again.

"How will you juggle fatherhood, working on the tree farm business and commuting to the lodge, Matt?" The question came from Jackson.

"I'm glad you asked, because I wanted to talk to Connor about that." Matt switched his attention from Jackson to Connor. "I don't know if you've figured out what to do now that you've separated from the air force, but I'm resigning from the lodge. I told Applegate I'd stay on until he hires and trains a replacement, and I was hoping you'd be interested."

"In running maintenance at the lake lodge?"

"Yeah. Lauren is still doing the website and managing reservations and such from home. I'm not sure how long she'll keep doing that after our peanut is born, but she says she'd like to try. But I can't keep doing the commute. I think you'd be a good fit, and you'd be as close to home as you are now, just on the other side of the mountains."

"Sadie still has a couple months of treatments."

"Right. Peanut's not due for nearly that. If you're interested, we should talk. Housing can be included—there's a cozy cabin that Applegate rents out right now, but he's willing to let it be employee housing, if his new hire has a family."

Wow. Talk about speaking peace into a storm. "I'll talk to Sadie." Connor leaned over, extending a hand toward Matt. Matt shook it and nodded.

Wow, Lord! It sounded like a promising possibility. A promising future for him and the ones he loved.

You sit enthroned as King forever.

He prayed that he'd remember this moment, this truth, in the harder days to come. Because there would be hard days, maybe even hard seasons. Things that might even break his heart—love came with that risk. But God was enthroned above all of it.

Ultimately, He was the good king. A very good king indeed.

Epilogue

(in which life is beautiful)

Crickets chirped into the calm evening, a cool breeze proclaiming the arrival of fall. Sadie slipped her arms into that oatmeal sweater her mom had given her and wrapped it tight around her body. As she moved toward the front door in search of Connor, the mirror near the coatrack snagged her attention.

Her pixie-cut hair was now over an inch long. She swiped at the bangs she styled to the side, tipped her head, and smiled. Short hair wasn't so bad, and she admitted that over the summer, not having the blanket of her long hair on her neck had been rather nice. Still, she was glad to see it growing back.

Mostly, she was glad treatment had been done. Relieved that the scans two weeks before had come back clean. And so thankful for the cancer that forced her to go back to Sugar Pine. Who would have thought that what she had then considered a death sentence had actually been her pathway to this new life?

You did, didn't You? She lifted her heart up to heaven with praise, reciting the verse Connor had shared with her back in May, after he and his brothers returned from their day on the ridge. Wow, had that day been one of surprises. Now, months later she and Connor were living in the most adorable cabin by Lake Tahoe, he was employed by the lodge where Matt and Lauren had fallen in love, and she was learning how to do some of what Lauren had done for Mr. Applegate so Lauren would have time with Fiona, Lauren and Matt's new baby girl.

Not how Sadie had pictured her life at all, and wasn't that perfectly amazing?

Pushing through the screen door that led to the deck, Sadie strode to the place Connor stood gazing up at the star-salted sky.

"Hi, handsome." She slipped her arms around his waist.

Connor welcomed her with a hug and a kiss to her short hair. "Where have you been all my life? Been standing here lonely. Missing you."

She snuggled into him, still amazed that the honor-bound and sort-of-serious Connor Murphy would say such sweet things to her. "I was just in there thinking."

"About what, hon?"

"That this life we have together, it's kind of beautiful. Just like you said it would be."

He turned her fully into his embrace and held her close. Like she was wanted and precious. "Yeah." He found her lips and lingered there for a moment. "I love this beautiful life with you."

The End

I hope you enjoyed Connor and Sadie's story and that it encouraged you to trust God's good plans, even when life looks grim. I'd so appreciate it if you'd leave your thoughts on the story in the form of a review on Amazon or Goodreads (or both!)

Also, there's more Murphy Brothers! Book #4, This Life, will be released in March, 2021. Reserve your copy today!

Made in the USA
Middletown, DE
11 November 2021